AiZ:
Alice in Zombieland

The Complete Saga

By Joshua Cook

ZombieACRES.com
Cafepress.com/ZombiesACRES
Facebook.com/ZombieACRES
Twitter.com/ZombieACRES

Edited by Julianne Snow

Copyright © 2011 Joshua Cook

Interior design by The Mad Formatter
www.TheMadFormatter.com

This book is protected under the copyright laws of the United States of America. Any reproduction or other unauthorized use of the material or artwork is strictly prohibited

ISBN-13: 978-1469903309

ISBN-10: 146990330X

For Briare Octavia
Welcome to the world
And thank you
For lighting up my life
Daddy Loves You

Table of Contents

The Interview 07

Mommy Deadest 13

Tough Love 21

The Boy Who Cried Zombie 31

No Place Like Home 39

Always and Forever 47

Taken 55

Loves Avenger 59

The Subject 65

Boy Meets Girl 71

Girl Meets Boy 77

Blake Island 81

Family Matters 87

Alice in Zombieland 93

The Interview

Television sets across America flicked on almost simultaneously. The country collectively held its breath out of sheer anticipation. Few times in America's history had one moment brought all her people together. This was one of those times. This moment would go down as one of the most important events in human history.

"Ladies and Gentlemen, do not adjust your television sets." The voice on the television was firm, yet possessed a calming quality, the hallmark of a veteran anchorman. "We are intentionally not revealing tonight's guest yet. With the amazing shock to the country that Mr. Lohman's buzz has already served to spawn, we thought it best to try and ease our viewers into what is about to come."

Tom Laudner finished speaking and the previously blank screens flashed to life, showing his face, but not that of his guest. "This interview is taking place at an undisclosed location for the safety and security of all who are involved. I am speaking with William Lohman, a former employee – of sorts – of Roslun Global. Within the last five years, Roslun has seen major growth and has become the leading pharmaceutical company in the United States. Mr. Lohman's recent announcement has helped to explain why."

The screen cut to black again and broadcast nothing but dead silence for almost two minutes. A collective nation held its breath yet again; imaginations ran wild in the heads of every man, woman, and child watching. Finally, Tom's face returned, and the sounds of last-second scuffling could be heard in the background. Tom glanced to one side, his eyes throwing an *"Are we back on?"* look at his producer. He gave a slight nod of acknowledgment to his unseen producer and turned his attention back to the camera, but before Tom could welcome the nation back to the broadcast, a sound came across the airwaves. It wasn't quite a voice, though words seemed to be carried by it.

"Hello." *Rusty.* That was the only way Bob Johns could describe what he heard in his Duluth living room that night.

"My name is William Lohman." *Hole.* A hole in your larynx, to be exact. That is how Phyllis Weidmar would later describe what she heard to her Wednesday bridge game in Miami.

Tom took back control of his broadcast. "Welcome, Mr. Lohman." Tom's butter-smooth voice set the viewers at ease, though not because of its perfectly groomed diction and pitch. That night it made people happy simply because it was not William Lohman's rasp. "We are going to pan over to Mr. Lohman in just a few seconds. I want to be perfectly clear on one matter, though." The camera zoomed in on Tom's eyes which expressed the gravity of the situation better than the words he uttered next. "What you are about to see is not for the squeamish. That cannot be emphasized enough. Please leave the room or turn the channel if you are afraid of what you may see."

The camera stayed focused on Tom, giving everyone ample time to ponder his warning. With a nod, Tom gave the cameraman the sign to pan over to the hot seat - ever so slowly. Sources have since claimed to have observed much vomiting for the remainder of the interview.

William Lohmans' skin was heavily blackened and blotchy, making it appear as if he had been on the losing end of an extremely bad beating. Around his eye sockets and orifices, the skin was sickly receded. Gashes along his neckline were partially draining a thick, dark fluid and had to be wiped every few minutes, drawing even more attention to the deep cuts around his throat. They looked to be made in haste, with many stops and starts. William's teeth seemed large in his mouth, next to the receding, blackened gums. On his head he wore an expensive looking fedora, which helped draw some attention away from the grotesqueness of his face.

Alice in Zombieland

"So why don't you begin to tell us what your announcement is, Mr. Lohman." Tom's voice came across the airwaves once again, but this time people were not as happy as they were still forced to stare at William Lohman's face of death.

"As you have said, Tom, I was formerly employed by the Roslun Corporation. I was their salesman for special projects. I was a shining specimen of their progress and was made to prove it in secret meetings all over the globe." The rasping voice coming out of that gut-wrenching face was worse than any horror film, yet his clothes seemed to match his salesman title - an expensive, dark suit with a bright red power tie. "As far back as the sixties, the powers that be have been seriously experimenting on ways to beat death. Their first breakthrough came in 1968, when they managed to partially reanimate a corpse. By partially, I mean that Specimen Zero could only wave his arms and legs; but the limbs were dead - and *moving* - nonetheless."

Camera 2 cut to Tom Laudner's face. Tom was a handsome man, but compared to William Lohman he was a *Greek God*. "What proof do you have that this *Specimen Zero* even existed? I find it hard to believe that, even back in the sixties, something this big would not have been leaked at some point."

"Oh it was leaked, Mr. Laudner." Lohman gave Tom a look like an adult gives a child when they are about to impart a life lesson; even through the oddly hanging skin and deathly pallor, that look was unmistakable. "And it was just as quickly covered up. Writer and director George Romero has become the *Father of the Modern Zombie*, and that is truer than most realize. Mr. Romero actually worked at an underground testing lab in Pennsylvania in 1968. That lab had managed to somehow *misplace* one of the observation videos from the night of Specimen Zero's second birth."

"George being the quickest on his toes that night proposed they film a cheesy horror movie to cover up these film reels of Specimen Zero. One month later, *Night of the Living Dead* was finished. What nobody ever expected was the success of this new genre, and the fascination of the American people with the idea of bringing the dead back to life.

"Now wait a second," Tom sounded a little agitated this time. "You expect me to swallow that... that... that *Night of the Living Dead* was a cover-up?" He spit out this last part like it was burning his throat.

"You may swallow whatever you wish, Mr. Laudner, I expect nothing. I am telling you the truth, and that is all." William was doing his best to smirk, but succeeded only in making his features more disgusting. "As I was saying, this rise, though unexpected, was a godsend for the Second Birth project, as it had come to be known. It enabled them to keep producing these low end horror films, which helped a little financially, but mostly it cast doubt on every single piece of evidence ever brought to light. With so many of these films coming out, and the technology so dated, there was no way to prove authenticity."

"So the Second Birth project just kept on going. The major players would switch every so-often, but the goals and practices would remain the same. With the boom of the pharmaceutical industry during the seventies, drug companies became more and more interested in the Second Birth technology. Roslun came into the game during the late eighties under the generic title Danko Drug Co., due to Civil Liberties protests and controversy surrounding Second Birth rumors. The early nineties brought an end to the rumors and provided the first concrete proof as technology finally reached the point to see through Second Birth's cover-ups once and for all."

"Mr. Lohman!" Tom almost screamed at his guest, his practiced air of composure definitely shaken. "I have been in the news for thirty years, and I have never heard any of this!"

"Have you never discovered new information years after the actions had taken place? I'm dead and even I understand how cover-ups work. It was decided in most of these cases that public safety was more important than public knowledge. After a particularly nasty incident, Danko Drug Co. was dissolved and Roslun emerged as themselves; quickly becoming a powerhouse in the Second Birth project. Roslun Global was the first one to bring Zombie A.C.R.E.S. to the idea table."

"Acres?"

"Animated Corpses Reintegration Experimental Subdivision. The Second Birth experiments have gotten to the point of actual moving and thinking zombies. Roslun wanted to take the experiments out of the underground labs and into a small gated-community. After much debate, and great monetary cost to Roslun, powerful benefactors were convinced of the merits of the program and Zombie A.C.R.E.S. was built in 2005 in the desert of Nevada."

"So for the last six years, there has been a zombie housing program in Nevada? And who are the major players involved in this Second Birth project? The government?"

"The government had knowledge and closely followed Second Birth, but I'm not aware of any government getting involved in any actions or projects."

"IMPOSSIBLE!" Tom screamed, his journalistic professionalism gone for the moment. "That's just outrageous! You're saying that *no* government had anything to do with these zombie projects and cover-ups?"

"Other than possessing knowledge of the program, I've never seen any government involvement. It may be hard to believe, but again, I'm just telling you the truth."

"So why have you decided to come forward now, six years after this all started? Did your conscience come back to life all of a sudden?"

"Yes."

"Yes?"

"Yes, that is exactly what happened. Before

2010, *zombies* could not feel." That word - *zombies* - came out even more heinous than most of William Lohman's words. "Early experiments only resulted in a lot of screaming from the zombies, whose ability to speak was just beginning. By summer 2010, feelings were brought back online, and things were smooth. The zombies said they only felt minimal pain, but there only seemed small traces of any indication to a conscience. This is when my second birth occurred. I had only been dead a week when I was discovered. At first, I felt nothing inside. Just empty. The more they toted me around, the more I learned. That is when I started to feel something: Anger. That was my first emotion. I wanted to get them for what they have done to us. How dare they play God?!"

"But these experiments are to ultimately help the living, aren't they?"

"At this point, who the hell knows? I have heard some talk of *helping people*, but much more it has been of war and weapons. Who knows where…"

Instant darkness. All of the video feeds carrying the simulcast went dead. After what felt like an eternity, two news anchors were smiling at the viewers.

"It seems there has been some technical difficulty with our live feed. We thank Tom and his… *guest*… for their time and work. We will keep you informed as this story unfolds. Tonight was unfolding well for these women as the annual Laundry Folding Competition was starting…"

Mommy Deadest

There was so much commotion Barbara was confused. She tried to sort out what had just happened; turning it over and over in her mind, but it was all such a jumble that she couldn't make either heads or tails of it. One minute they were doing routine testing on one of the experiments, the next Barbara was dodging security on the way out.

Roslun Global wanted her to stay at work and receive the medical attention they provided, but Barbara knew all too well what Roslun's idea of medical attention was. She wanted none of it. She was scratched, and badly. There was only one cure for that in the company's eye...Death followed by incineration.

I have a family to worry about. I can't let them kill me.

This thought stayed with Barbara for the rest of her life.

The temperature was cool and a nice breeze was coming in off the Puget Sound as Barbara sped down the road. Even with the mild Seattle weather, she was sweating like a fat man in summertime. Barbara's normally full and luscious red hair was being held to her face in tight clumps by the sweat pouring down her face.

Just stress. Too soon for symptoms. Not even an hour has passed yet.

Just a few minutes later, the red Camry came to a screeching halt in its driveway. As she got out of the car, Barbara noticed that almost every light in the house was on. This was not unusual for her family. She was always telling them she should have stock in the electric company with all the lights they leave on. A slight smile broke through Barbara's face as memories of her children and husband flashed through her mind.

Quickly pushing these memories aside, Barbara rushed up the front walk towards the front door. As she burst through, Barbara screamed, "Josh! Alice!" She knew her workaholic husband Michael was out of town on business, so she just needed to find the kids. "Where are you guys?!"

"Yeah?" Josh called from down the hall.

Barbara ran to her son's room to find the eight-year-old playing his Nintendo Wii. "You need to get dressed. We have to go." Barbara told the shaggy haired kid on the floor.

"Why? Where are we going?" There was the slightest hint of a whine in Josh's voice. He had finally defeated the second-to-last level boss in his game, but he hadn't saved his progress yet.

"Just get ready. Where's your sister?"

"I'm right here. What are we getting ready for?" A girl's voice came from the doorway, startling Barbara.

As Alice walked into the room, her mother reeled on her. "Don't ask questions. Pack lightly. Now."

"What's wrong with your leg?" Alice pointed at Barbara's thigh, which was now leaking bright red down her leg. "Why's it bleeding like that?"

Barbara looked down at her leg. She wrapped it the best she could when she was driving here, but the bandages weren't holding very well. Even as she stared down at the blood escaping from her body, one thought echoes through Barbara's mind. *The blood is still flowing. That's a good sign at least.*

"An accident at work." Barbara forced a thin smile, trying to set the kids at ease, even if just slightly.

"Is that why we're running?"

Alice was only sixteen, but more like her mother than even she realized; both in physical appearance and personality. Barbara was not a woman to take things at face value, a trait which was passed onto her daughter. When Barbara saw Alice with the same look Barbara got when she meant business, she knew it was time to level with her.

"Something went wrong at work." Barbara started slowly, trying to remain as calm as she could. With wavering words, she continued, "Roslun deals with some very impor-

Alice in Zombieland

tant, but also very dangerous, science."

"I've been online, Mom. I know what people say goes on in that *office* of yours."

"I haven't. What goes on at your work, Mommy?" asked an innocent voice from the floor.

Barbara and Alice had both forgotten about Josh, who was packing up the essentials for the impromptu trip: his Pikachu pillow pal, the autographed Griffey Jr. Mariners ball cap he got last summer with his dad, and the three packages of fruit snacks he had been squirreling in his room, in case he ever needed a midnight snack.

"Nothing, Josh. We just test things to make the world better." Barbara peered into Josh's Spider-man backpack. "Be sure to pack some t-shirts and underwear. Alice, let's go to your room and get you ready."

Barbara turned and had to steady herself on Josh's dresser. She walked from the room, but began to stagger as she left the room. Barbara had the chills and aches all over, yet her clothes and skin were soaked. Holding onto the wall for support, she tried to make it to Alice's room.

Alice couldn't stand to see her mother in this much agony, so she slipped under Barbara's arm and helped her into the bedroom. Once inside, Barbara collapsed onto the bed. Alice ran from the room and quickly returned carrying clean bandages and gauze.

Barbara was sprawled out on Alice's bed with her red hair flowing around her. An aura of pink surrounded her entire body as her blood mixed with her sweat. Alice began to remove the old bandages when her arm was slapped away hard.

"Don't!" Barbara screamed, but quickly subdued her voice and continued, "I'm not sure exactly how this spreads. Coming home put you guys at risk as it is, but I had to say good bye."

"Good bye?!" The voice that Alice emitted was shocked, but somewhere inside her a voice had already told her that

Barbara would not be making this trip.

"Yes." Barbara's voice was barely over a whisper. "I was scratched at work today."

"Scratched? By what?"

"An experiment." Barbara grimaced hard as pain ripped through her body. "I'm going to be dead soon. You have to lis-"

"Dead?!" Alice was in shock. This was her mother, the woman that had raised her since birth. Now she was telling her that she would soon be dead. "This makes no sense. What experiments were you working on?"

"I'm just an assistant, you know that." Barbara tried to sit up, but sloshed back into her pink aura. "I don't know exactly what was going on tonight, but the subject we were working with was no ordinary woman."

"But why are you *dying*?!"

Barbara struggled with telling her sixteen-year-old daughter the truth. Alice should be going out with her friends, not having to watch her mother slowly die in front of her. The unfortunate truth was that there was not much time left before Roslun Global sent a cleanup crew to grab Barbara and *contain* any potential outbreak. She was dead either way, and she knew it.

"We have brought the dead back to life." *So blunt.* Even as the words left Barbara's mouth, they sounded outright absurd to her. If only there were time to ease Alice into this. "I know this is a lot to handle, but there is not much time."

"Bullshit! You mean like zombies or somethin'?!" Alice could not believe what she was hearing. Zombies existed, but they didn't exist in *her* life. They were only in news reports and internet videos.

"That is exactly what I mean, Alice." Barbara's green eyes were more serious than Alice had ever seen them. This look scared Alice. This look scared her more than the sight of her mother dying. "One of them scratched me pretty bad. There is nothing that can be done to save me. You have got

Alice in Zombieland

to listen to me now."

Alice didn't want to listen; she wanted to be held. She wanted her mother to just get up, wrap her leg, and hug her tightly. However, that was the wishful thinking of a scared little girl, something that could never come true anymore, and Alice realized that fact. "OK. I'm listening."

"Good." A smile stretched across Barbara's face, but only for a moment. "You have to get Josh and get out of here."

"Where do we go?"

"Doesn't matter. Roslun Global will be looking for me."

"Shouldn't you let them help you?" There was a hint of hope in Alice's question, but her mother quickly quelled that.

"They will not help us! You are to run far away from them, Alice! Do you hear me?! Don't trust them!"

Her mother's sudden outburst caused all of Alice's pent up tension to burst and she started to cry. She couldn't help it. It wasn't even the screaming that bothered her most; that was just the final straw. It was the way her mother looked that bit away at her the hardest.

The pink aura that once was almost beautiful had become much redder now, in strong contrast to Barbara's utterly pale complexion. Her flowing, red hair had become intertwined with itself, causing gnarls and tangles. The *scratch* her mother claimed to have gotten has almost stopped gushing blood and the surrounding skin had turned the blackness of death.

"What about Dad?" Alice cried to her mother. "Can't he help us?"

"I don't know. You can try, but don't rely on it. The world is tough, and that means you have to be tougher. Get Josh and get out of here. Do you understand me?"

Even at sixteen, Alice was mature enough to understand what was happening. The world had become a different place since the Lohman interview, and everybody had to grow up a little faster. Those that didn't ended up dead or on one of those news reports (or both). "Okay, Mom. I understand."

"I love you, Alice."

Alice embraced her mother as she whispered in her ear. "I love you, too, Mom."

Barbara never got to hear her daughter tell her she loved her for the last time. Death had taken her, relaxing her pain and fever-twisted features into a more peaceful mask of stillness. Alice's tears spilled even faster. She couldn't stop crying, even when Josh walked into the room.

"Mom, I'm ready." Josh saw his mother lying on the bed, her eyes open, so he hopped up on the bed with her. Alice couldn't stop him before he landed on his mother's body.

Barbara's body just lay there, cooling rapidly. Even when Josh started shaking her to wake her up, his mother's body remained motionless. Alice grabbed her brother and yanked him off the bed.

"What's wrong with Mom?" Josh glanced back at Barbara's corpse and Alice turned his face towards her own.

Looking straight into his innocent brown eyes, Alice simply said, "Josh, Mom is dead." *So blunt.* She had wanted to ease him into the idea, but the sense of urgency hung heavy in the air. There was no time to waste. Her mom said to run, so they had to run.

After covering Barbara's body up with a blanket, Alice tore through her room stuffing items into a backpack. Josh sat at the foot of the bed and cried for his mother. "I know you're sad, Little Man, but you need to be brave. Mom told me you have to be strong and take care of me now, okay? Josh, look at me. We need to get going."

Josh nodded his understanding through his tears. Alice knew he was in shock, but she also knew there was nothing she could do about it at this moment. She helped him up and they hurried into the kitchen. She searched every drawer and cupboard for a flashlight. Finally she found one in the cupboard above the fridge. Alice grabbed a chair and pulled it over to the fridge, making loud skipping noises the whole way. She climbed on top of it and reached for the flashlight.

"Mom!" Josh yelled.

Alice wheeled around, almost falling off the chair. In the doorway to the kitchen stood Barbara, but something about her was odd. There was no love in her eyes anymore. Those green eyes used to be so full of life, but that was gone; in its place was the milky white void of nothingness.

"Josh! Don't!" Alice screamed and jumped for Josh but it was too late. Josh had already reached his mother, hugging her legs triumphantly.

"I knew you would be okay." He grinned from ear to ear as he gazed up at his mother.

Barbara slowly looked down at Josh. For the first time he noticed the drool hanging from her mouth. Josh tried to run but Barbara grabbed his arm, snarling as she pulled him to her. He screamed as his mother lifted him up and took a large bite out of his left arm, spraying blood around the room like a sprinkler.

Alice was on top of them in a flash and shoved her mother hard. Barbara stumbled, dropping Josh as she bounced off the wall. He popped up as only little kids can and ran to Alice.

His arm was bad; Alice could see muscle and what she thought might be bone through all the gore. She grabbed a towel from the counter and attempted to wrap it up. Josh needed medical help, but for now she had to get them out of here. Backpack in hand, she guided Josh through the patio doors and into the backyard. They were halfway across the yard when Alice remembered the flashlight was still in the kitchen. She had dropped it in the scuffle and would have to go back for it.

"You wait here. I'll be right back."

Alice gave Josh the backpack and ran back into the

kitchen. She stopped short when she saw her mother walking toward her. Barbara's mouth was in an eternal snarl and still had bits of Josh's flesh dangling from it. Instead of emptiness, Alice now sensed hunger.

Alice knew the flashlight was a lost cause. She turned into the backyard, and slammed the glass patio door behind her. Barbara walked into the glass door and stumbled backwards. She walked into the door again and again, her hands constantly reaching out for Alice and Josh.

Alice pulled her cell phone from her back pocket and keys a few buttons. Her father may be gone on business, but there was one person that was still around. "Hello? Gee? Something's wrong…We need you…Hurry…"

Alice's plea into her cell phone was cut short as Barbara's relentless pursuit through the patio doors finally paid off. The glass doors shattered into thousands of glinting shards that went flying in every direction. Barbara's face and body were badly cut, but she continued on her course without ever missing a beat.

Alice turned and ran toward the garage. She reached the door before she realized Josh was not with her. She looked back to see him standing there, frozen with fear. "Josh! Run!"

Alice ran for Josh, but again she was too late. Before she could ever hope to reach him, Barbara had her young son in her mouth once again. Another bite came, this time from the boy's jugular. Blood poured from his throat in a crimson river.

"NO! Josh… No!"

Tough Love

"NO! Josh... No!"

Georgia Marie heard the screams by the time she reached the Saunders' house. Gee was more than half a block from the house, so she kicked it into high gear and sprinted the rest of the way. As she came around the corner of the garage and entered the backyard, she immediately saw the reason for Alice's hysterics.

Barbara was gnawing on Josh's neck. Blood poured from the child's lifeless body until Barbara finally dropped him. Gee had to look away. Even though she was not blood related to Barbara, the whole scene was too much for her to handle. Her attention then turned to her step sister.

I'm gonna have to handle this; Alice is a basket case.

Gee felt terrible for having little compassion for Barbara and Josh, but it was too late for them. She knew what had to be done and she knew Alice would be of little help in her current state. She struggled to block who the dead bodies used to be from her mind. Memories like the day Barbara married Gee's father, Josh's last birthday party with the Spider-Man theme, and last Christmas Eve when Barbara had read *'Twas the Night before Christmas*, as was her family's tradition before marrying Gee's father, still ran through her head.

Focus, girl! That's all gone now and Alice needs you.

"Alice!" Gee screamed, trying to cut through the images of carnage as Barbara tore another flap of skin from Josh's neck, this one ripping free only after it had taken his cheek with it. "Alice! I need you to listen to me! Do exactly as I say!" She whipped her red flannel shirt off, waving it wildly in the air in an attempt to get Alice's eyes off of her mother, who was ready for her next snack.

Am I even reaching through to that little brat? Do I ever?!

Again, Gee felt horrible about her detachment from her

father's new family and her animosity toward Alice. How could she even be thinking such terrible thoughts right now? Just because Alice was not her blood sister didn't mean she deserved *this*.

Georgia Marie was not a particularly fit girl; she was naturally thin, despite rarely exercising and typically eating junk food, as most college students do. She had, however, taken gymnastics back in elementary school and had learned to maneuver her small frame quickly; she hoped muscle memory and instinct would kick in and allow her to move with agility for the next few minutes.

"Alice! I'm coming to save you, but you need to calm down and listen to me! Look at me, Alice!" Something finally clicked in Alice's head and Gee's voice made it through. Alice turned and met Gee's eyes, which were a steely, cold gray under her short brown hair. "Great! Thank you, Alice. Now listen carefully and do exactly as I say. Crawl under the table to your right. Go quick!"

Luckily Alice, whose gaze had shifted to the patio table, did not see what Gee saw. Alice's mother…well the dead, rotting shell formerly known as her mother, was lurching mere inches behind Alice. A cold and sickly-looking hand was reaching, clawing, just behind the trailing of Alice's long, red hair.

"Alice, I need you to move faster." Gee tried to remain calm, remembering herself at Alice's age: though it was only three years ago, it felt like a lifetime had elapsed since then.

There is no way I would have been able to make it through any of this at sixteen.

Alice may have just been a kid in Gee's mind, but suddenly Gee realized just how much mental toughness her little sister possessed. Regardless, Alice wasn't going to make it; Barbara was closing on her. Gee decided to pull on her big girl panties and make sure Alice had all the time she needed to get out of the death trap she was in.

Alice in Zombieland

As Alice was still crawling toward the patio table, Gee grabbed the first thing she saw, a lawn gnome, and threw it into the side of Barbara's head. This blow only managed to daze the undead monster momentarily. As this former husk of Barbara spun and flailed her arms, she knocked over the table Alice was crawling toward. It hit the concrete patio with an ear-splitting *CLANG* which brought Alice even farther out of her shocked daze. She got to her feet and ran behind the upturned patio table, which had skittered across the concrete and was rolling from side to side on its round edge, much like the Weeble Woobles Alice played with as a child.

With her sister out of harm's way, Gee knew it was time to finish this and get out of dodge. She scanned the backyard for more of the undead. She had been so focused on Alice's immediate situation that it hadn't occurred to her that more of the creatures could be lurking around. Luckily there was only Alice's now dead mother to contend with.

I coulda taken her when she was alive.

This thought actually made Gee laugh, which Alice must have thought a bit strange. Gee searched the chaos of the backyard for anything to be used as a weapon. Time was running out, and Gee knew she had to strike soon.

That was when a broken piece of fence was spotted, but not by Gee. Alice had spotted the piece of fence and noted the extremely sharp point the break made. Alice sprang up and grabbed hold of her newly found weapon.

"Alice! No!" Gee screamed, attempting to stop Alice as she ran full speed at her mother. The sharp, splintered end of the fence board was held high over her head, ready to be thrust into its target.

Without missing a step, Alice leapt from a chair and flew through the air. It was like a scene from an action movie: Alice flying through the air, weapon on target, aimed straight at her mother's temple. Gee saw it all in slow-motion and she would later run the scene over and over in her head, mainly because everything went along great – until the landing. The wooden missile found its mark flawlessly, but Alice's momentum carried her body into her mother's. The collision flipped Alice backward onto the electric grill, knocking her unconscious. She slid off the chrome lid of the grill and slumped on the patio.

Gee ran to Alice, praying she was still alive. Tears stung her eyes as she scooped up her sister's limp body and checked for signs of life. After finding a pulse and feeling Alice's breathing, Gee was able to think more clearly. Her first priority was finding a safe spot to rest and helping Alice heal enough to move on her own again.

How the hell did Barbara become a zombie? Her job? Could the tabloids be telling the truth? Is Roslun Global responsible for the outbreaks?

Zombies had become a fact of life nine years ago when a man by the name of William Lohman had shocked the nation by revealing he was a true to life zombie. He had accused Roslun Global of doing all kinds of experiments with the goal of bringing the dead back to life. This news lit up the conspiracy sites around the world, and thrust Roslun Global to the forefront of controversy and media attention.

Barbara worked at Roslun. Something must've gone wrong.

There had been scattered outbreaks of zombie activity since Lohman revealed his side of the story. They were usually small and quickly contained, many with no physical evidence left behind. The media was often too late to report anything other than after-the-fact eyewitness accounts and hearsay, but a few had been documented. Zombie surveillance websites, tracking attacks and other related events, had popped up like daisies; lots of people checked them as regularly as they did the weather. School kids were taught to look both ways before crossing the street *and* to look out the window before going outside. The attacks had been so few and far between, though, that most people regarded zombies as something akin to rabid dogs; they were dangerous and real, but so rare that they could be confined to the back of

Alice in Zombieland

one's mind.

Where there's one, there's more. There's always more.

There was a small abandoned house a few blocks away where Gee used to go to smoke a joint after school. She hoped it hadn't been overrun by zombies, or worse, junkies. The fact was Alice's home was just not safe anymore.

Having grown up in the Age of the Zombie, Gee knew what needed to be done. She pulled the fence board out of Barbara's head, finding a sick gratification at the squishing sound it made as it overcame the suction of the wound, and headed for her step brother.

Gotta make sure he's dead... For good.

Gee stood over her little brother's body. Even though Josh and Alice weren't her full blood siblings, Gee had always thought of them as her little brother and sister. The tears came and she was powerless to stop them. She waited, watching for any movement through the blurry lens of her tears... Nothing.

Still better safe than sorry.

Gee tightened her grip on the fence board and braced for what she must do. She took a deep breath to steady herself and, without hesitating, she stabbed the sharp wood through her little brother's head and fell to her knees, sobbing uncontrollably.

As she rose to her feet, wiping tears and blood from her face, Gee surveyed the devastation that surrounded her. At her feet lay the dead body of Josh, an innocent child. Barbara, once a loving mother and wife, was now a corpse, skull fragments and blood surrounding her. Young Alice's life was still in trouble. There was no fairness in any of it. The anger over the injustices swelled inside Gee until she could not resist one last kick to the side of Barbara's bloody head.

You caused this. I only wish you could feel the pain.

Gee mustered her remaining strength and decided it was time for them to move. Alice was still unconscious on the patio, so Gee picked her up and carried her inside the house.

She reached for the patio door out of habit, but realized it was already closed. It had been shattered, and Gee shivered a little when she guessed how.

Gee lowered her sister gently to the kitchen floor and began to search for some necessities for the road. Luckily, most of the items she needed were right there in the kitchen; flashlight (which was on the floor in the corner instead of its normal spot in the cupboard above the fridge), hammer, a few cans of food, and some bottled water. There was one more thing, but she had to run upstairs to grab it.

Once upstairs, Gee jogged into the guest bedroom. Whenever she came to visit, this was her Fortress of Solitude. Things got tense sometimes with her dad always working, and this was the only escape she had. *That's being polite about it, Gee.* This thought lingered in her mind for a moment as she crossed over to the window.

Normally this view was as beautiful and peaceful as any street in America. Things now took on a sinister tone. The trees that lined either side of the street played with the lights, casting dark shadows on the ground. Moving in and out of these shadows were a few of the neighbors. Instead of waving and greeting each other, these once happy neighbors were now shambling aimlessly along the street.

I knew it – there had to be more of them, but why?

Gee opened the bottom drawer of the dresser, rummaged at the back of it, and grabbed her weed kit. If this was the end of the world, she'd need it.

Alice was still out cold when Gee got back to the kitchen. She looked at her little pile of supplies and realized she couldn't carry her sister and the survival gear. She stole a quick glance into the back yard. The coast was clear. She headed to the garage. At the very front, behind a couple of boxes of random junk, stood what Gee was looking for; Barbara's mountain bike with the Burley kid trailer still attached. It hadn't been used in years, but the tires were still full of air. Barbara had been big on exercising when Josh was younger, but that hadn't lasted long. Gee maneuvered the bike past the boxes, tapped the garage door opener, tossed the big crowbar that had been her dad's in the trailer, and rolled the bike and trailer into the driveway.

The sun was beginning to set. Gee ran into the kitchen and scooped Alice up. She carried the teenage girl out to the bike, and laid her in the trailer, gently kissing her forehead and wiping the red hair from her face. After grabbing the supplies and setting them alongside her sister, Gee hopped on the bike and peddled toward the only refuge she could think of.

The empty house seemed eerily quiet when they got there, though most old houses were eerie at night. Gee stashed the bike and Alice's trailer in some bushes near the house. If this outbreak gets out of hand, she didn't want people to know anyone was here. She grabbed the flashlight and crowbar and peered into the windows.

I don't see anyone, alive or dead, but that doesn't mean much. I'm surprised there isn't more activity; it looks like somebody has actually bought the place in the last couple years.

Gee tried the front door. It was unlocked. She made a quick run through of the whole first floor. Nothing seemed disturbed; no signs of the undead or destruction. It wasn't like there was much to take. The front room and dining room had a few random pieces of furniture, most of which would be too large to be practical on the move. The kitchen was pretty bare as well, but the cabinet drawers were scattered on the floor.

I'm glad to know I haven't fallen into the Twilight Zone at some point. Somebody was here and took what they needed. Maybe they haven't left...

Gee crept to a staircase at the front of the house. Quietly moving up the staircase, she steadied herself, ready to attack at the first sign of movement – whatever the cause may be. When she reached the top of the stairs, she saw there were only two bedrooms and a bathroom along the dark hallway.

She easily cleared bedroom one as it was completely empty and didn't even have a closet. Heading a little further down the hall, she started to smell something. After searching the bathroom, she walked toward the bedroom at the end of the hall. The wind outside picked up, carrying a pungent odor into her nose.

Gee knew that smell. It was rancid and her stomach suddenly felt like it wanted to turn itself inside-out. Flashlight in one hand, crowbar in the other, Gee slowly opened the bedroom door with her foot, heart pounding with the fear of what she may find.

As soon as the door creaked open, the smell of death slapped Gee in the face. The source of the smell was immediately located near the window, which was unfortunately closed. In a couple of armchairs sat the bodies of an elderly couple, both with gunshot wounds to the head.

Poor couple. Murder-suicide. Looks like the wife was bitten, which makes the husband the gunman for both. This could not have been caused by Barbara.

Gee walked slowly out of the room, wondering if she would have been able to do the same in the husband's place. By the time she got downstairs, nighttime was fully upon them. She needed to grab Alice and bring her into the safety of the house, even if it was just for the night.

After setting up a makeshift bed out of some old, and only mildly disgusting, blankets and laying Alice down, Gee went about boarding up the first floor windows. The furniture that was too heavy to be stolen was perfect to secure the place for now. After what seemed like the whole night to Gee, the first floor was secure enough for them.

It's not like I'm gonna be sleeping anyway.

As she sat cross-legged on the floor, holding Alice and just trying to absorb everything that had happened in the past few hours, Gee lost it. She screamed and sobbed, rocked back and forth, all the while holding her little sister in her arms. Gee's body was shaking so much from all the emotions that she didn't even notice when Alice first started moving.

"Alice! You're awake!" Every single thought left Georgia Marie's mind in an instant. The tears came on worse than they ever had, but they felt different – almost good. "No matter what, I will protect you from this point on...I promise!"

Gee hugged Alice tightly, holding her against her chest. As she brushed some dirt off of Alice's arm, Gee's mind once again went instantly blank...

No...How? You were fine...Maybe the scratch isn't from your mother.

On Alice's arm was a bright red scratch, completely contrasted against her milky, white skin. Gee examined the scratch closer. It was just as she feared. The edges of the scratch were already forming blackened edges.

Only a scratch. I have a little time before I have to...Well, before it's time to say goodbye.

The Boy Who Cried Zombie

The sound of gunshots was more deafening than the screams and groans of the undead. The resulting spray of blood as his bullets found their target, each one ripping through blackened and rotting flesh, was beautiful. The sound his footsteps made through the gory mess on the ground was sickening, but also satisfying. Sam was surrounded and low on ammo. He was not sure what he was going to do... then the beeping...

Burritos are done.

Sam paused his game and went into the kitchen to grab his food. The kitchen was a disaster and he knew he would never hear the end of it if his fiancée came home and saw this mess. There was a *discussion* about it earlier, as Sam remembered it. That was a couple hours ago, before Heather left for her Girl's Night.

With that *discussion* fresh in his mind, Sam hurriedly ate his burritos, barely taking time to enjoy them. Then, controller in hand, he found the next save point in his game and powered down. At a loss for where to start, he walked his plate back into the kitchen, knocking over a pile of pizza boxes on his way.

Ah, Zombie Fest. Sam got a fond look in his eyes and drifted away on memories of hanging out with his friends, eating pizza and watching the end of the world, due to the zombie apocalypse of course, over and over again. *We must have watched ten movies that night.* He absently rubbed his hands on his head, as if he were trying to run his fingers through his short, unkempt dark hair. He chuckled, but then remembered the one thing worse than a zombie apocalypse.

Better get this over with so we don't upset her highness.

Looking at Heather's innocent face, with her brown eyes that melt like chocolate, and a smile to light even the darkest abyss, one would never guess the emotional demons that seem to linger within. Even with her emotional baggage, Sam loved her more than life itself.

Sam gathered up the pizza boxes and the rest of the garbage around the apartment, and headed outside to throw it all in the dumpster. Wearing his normal, lazy attire of jeans and a novelty t-shirt (today was an old *Boondock Saints* shirt), he really did not feel like going through the hassle of finding socks and shoes and putting them on, so he decided to just run outside barefoot.

As he was outside attempting to shove his garbage into an already overflowing dumpster, something caught Sam's attention at the end of the alley. He noticed a guy slowly walking, or maybe shambling would be more accurate, down the alleyway. The term shambling popped into Sam's head because of the way the man's right leg was limp and slightly dragging behind him.

Is that what I think it is?!

Alarmed, Sam threw the last of the pizza boxes on the ground and bolted for the apartment. *I knew we should have gotten a second floor apartment in case the worst happens!* He ran straight to the computer, and logged into his most trusted zombie outbreak site to check for any recent activity. Since they have just moved to the Everett area, Sam kept it bookmarked to always be prepared. *Just like 'The Guide' tells us to.* It confirmed that there has been zombie activity in the area recently, but it looked to be localized and contained.

Being a good citizen, and a little too scared to run out attacking zombies just yet, Sam called the Zombie Emergency Hotline, which was apparently too busy with this *localized and contained* outbreak to show up in less than an hour.

Zombies move slowly, but they don't move that slow. And this place is like a buffet, all these apartments crammed on the first floor.

A new thought popped into Sam's head now. If this really was a dangerous outbreak, and they really did pick a zombie deathtrap as housing, then maybe they are really in

Alice in Zombieland

trouble. He grabbed his phone and frantically texted Heather:

Zombie comin. 4 real this time. R U ok? B ready. On my way.

No reply. After a few minutes he re-sent the text. Still no reply.

Typical. She's probably still pissed at me.

Sam ran outside, still barefoot, and saw Dirty Leg Dragger (Sam always had a thing for nicknames) still shambling up the alleyway. *This is it!* Sam had been waiting for an outbreak of his own for so long. This whole zombie mess started when he was pretty young, but growing up with zombies in the news had made Sam somewhat of a fanatic, to say the least.

Knowing his escape plan to the letter, Sam ran in the house and dug around for socks and shoes, figuring now was not the time to be lazy. He rushed down the hall and started grabbing tools from different parts of the room. Sam paused as he dug a small lockbox out of his sock drawer and unlocked it.

"I hoped I would never have to use you."

He knew this was a lie even as he said it aloud, but he thought it sounded cool to say. He pulled the small, snub-nosed revolver out of the lock box and slipped it in his pocket. It was an impulse buy at the pawn shop a few months back, after the clerk told him this would be all the firepower he would need. After grabbing a hunting knife and his black Skid-Lid helmet, complete with flames on the side, he ran out the door. Throwing on the helmet, Sam hopped onto his *chariot*, a baby blue moped with chrome finish.

I have to save my Heather... My future!

Even with his ride sounding like a hover vehicle straight out of *The Jetson's*, Sam felt brave. He knew this was his day. He *will* be a hero today.

When he pulled into Tasha's driveway to pick Heather

up, he slowly walked around, looking the neighboring houses up and down. Tasha's neighbors did not appreciate this as much as Sam would have liked, and he moved along back to Tasha's house after a few too many yells of "Creep" and "Pervert."

Tasha opened the door and rolled her eyes. "Heather, it's your…" she looked Sam up and down with distaste, "*worse* half." She stepped aside to let him in.

He found Heather and pulled her aside. He proceeded to tell her about Dirty Leg Dragger and the reported zombie activity. Sam was talking so fast even his own fiancée had a hard time making words out.

"Honey, I need you to slow down. I can't understand you." Heather said in a smooth and calm voice.

After explaining things at a slower pace, even if only a little slower, Heather finally started to understand what he was rambling on about.

"So you came rushing over here, gun in hand mind you, busting into our Girl's Night to cry zombie… Again? What the hell is your problem?"

"Yeah! What the hell *is* your problem?!" A third voice bellowed from the doorway.

They both look back at the bathroom door, which they thought was closed. There stood Tasha, her arms folded, long blonde hair lying over them. "I don't appreciate you barging in like this, with some bullshit story about zombies!"

"You know they're real. They're on the damn news for Christ's sake!" Sam yelled.

"I never said they weren't real, we just don't have them around here. That's why I moved here."

"That's how outbreaks happen… you don't know there's a weekend scientist trying to re-animate the dead down the road… Until he makes one mistake and all hell breaks loose for a few days."

Heather had had enough of their childish bickering.

Alice in Zombieland

"Fine. Let's go, Sam."

Tasha looked from Heather to Sam, and then back to Heather. "Why?"

"I love Sam. If he is this adamant that this could be an outbreak, I believe him." This was said more for Sam's good than it being the actual truth. Really, she just figured better safe than sorry, and this way she wouldn't have to listen to Sam all night.

"And so you two are just going to escape on his *bad-ass* bike out there?" Tasha pointed back at Sam's *chariot* with her thumb. "I don't think you guys are gonna get very far in this *major outbreak*." She started to laugh.

"Then we borrow your car."

Tasha stopped laughing and looked at Heather, "Over my dead body."

"If I'm right, that can be easily arranged." Sam mumbled under his breath.

Tasha shot Sam a dirty look and fixed her gaze back on Heather. "Seriously, that car goes nowhere without me. It may be a piece of shit, but it's my piece of shit."

"I don't care who comes. We need to go. This dicking around here is wasting too much time. Where are your keys?" Sam had already begun searching the nearest drawer for any keys he could find.

"They're in my purse. I'll grab them. Just stay out of my drawers."

"Gladly," Sam ignored yet another dirty look and began speaking more stridently. "Heather, get your stuff together and grab the bag off my bike. Tasha, I'm gonna grab a few supplies from around here."

"No you're not." Tasha's voice carried from down the hall.

"Fine. We die, it's on you." Sam yelled back.

"That is a chance I am willing to take."

"Well I'm not...." Sam grabbed the keys out of Tasha's hand as she walked back into the front hallway. "If I'm not grabbing supplies, I'm driving." He ran out the door before she had a chance to argue.

"He's a good driver, Tasha. Calm down." The look in Tasha's eyes told Heather her feeble attempt to calm the situation hadn't done much good.

They all piled into Tasha's Ford Escort, with the car's owner grudgingly taking the backseat. Sam started the car and pulled out of the driveway, heading towards I-5. Once they hit the interstate, he took the north on-ramp, hoping to head for Canada.

One of Sam's zombie sites had said there was a defense camp set up just on the other side of the border. Well off the beaten path, defense camps such as these were somewhat common and set up to help victims of a zombie attack or outbreak, but not run by any government organization. This information was kept from the girls since Sam knew they would consider the camp to be full of conspiracy theory *freaks*.

Sam instead used the time they had in the car spouting off zombie facts and survival tips the whole way north. He was so engrossed in helping *educate* the girls that he did not notice the occasional eye rolls, which were mostly coming from Tasha. A few miles out of town, Tasha had finally had enough and demanded to know where they are going.

Sam looked down and noticed the gas light had come on. "Not much further if we don't get some gas... So who's paying?"

The next exit brought the Ford Escort to a small, isolated gas station. It was almost pitch black, with the only light coming from two weak lamps by the gas pumps. Sam got out and began to pump the gas. After he was finished, he took munchie requests, along with Heather's debit card, and headed into the gas station.

"You don't look like a *Heather* to me, sir."

Sam finished setting his armful of stuff on the counter. "Seriously, dude? We're gonna do this now? I'm in a hurry,

Alice in Zombieland

just run the card so I can get outta here."

"What? Did somebody die?" The clerk laughed.

"They will soon, so hurry up."

Sam looked around nervously in a way that made the clerk feel uneasy. He swiped the card through the reader, but before he even had a chance to hand it back to Sam, a scream pierced the still air of the night. Both men jumped and looked out the large window.

Heather was struggling with someone near the back of the car. Sam knew this was no normal person and ran outside, leaving the food and card behind. The clerk watched as Sam darted out to the commotion.

Sam pulled out his revolver and quickly fired a shot at the zombie. The shot went wide and hit the gas pump, almost ricocheting into Heather. *Not like the video games, is it, Sam?* He steadied himself and tried again, this time hitting the zombie in the shoulder.

Heather broke free and ran to hide behind Sam, unsure of who was more dangerous at this point. Sam took aim and fired another shot, finally hitting their attacker in the face. The man fell to the ground as Sam's arm fell to his side.

With everything going on, Sam hadn't even noticed Heather still screaming behind him. Sam whirled around to notice another zombie. This one was busy ripping Tasha apart with his mouth, which kept him quiet enough for Sam to not notice at first. As Sam signaled for Heather to be quiet, he slowly walked around the car. Tasha's body lay half out of the car, her head almost touching the ground. The zombie was kneeling over her, munching on her flesh like a juicy red watermelon on a warm summer day.

The sight of the zombie tearing Tasha apart and her looking so... *dead*, was too much for Sam's stomach to handle. He bent over and threw up, the sloshing sound attracting the zombie's attention to the possibility of a new meal.

When Sam looked up, the zombie was almost on him. He quickly straightened up and fired his revolver, hitting his target squarely in the left eye. He ran back to Heather, hugging her and making sure she was ok. She nodded, saying she was, though talking was hard from the adrenaline she had pumping through her system.

"You... were... right."

"I'll gloat about it later. Right now we have to get out of here." He looked around, making sure there were no other zombies in the vicinity. With the coast being clear, he grabbed the corpse from the backseat. As he went to throw it to the ground, he noticed that it was a fresh zombie. The skin is still tight, with very little decomposition. He ran back to the first zombie and noticed the same thing.

Fresh zombies? Odd. Amateur scientists can't afford fresh corpses like these.

Sam snapped back from his thoughts and remembered one very important rule he had forgotten about. He ran back around to the driver's side of the car and gave Tasha two quick, close range, shots to the head and threw her body on the ground. Unfortunately, in his haste, he did not plan on the mess that would be left in the backseat as a result of his double-tap.

He grabbed Heather, who was still dazed, but a little more in control now, and started digging in the trunk for some blankets. Once they found a couple, they threw them over the bits of Tasha that were still left in the backseat, and started driving back towards I-5.

Just a little way down the road, Sam noticed a delivery truck on the side of the road that had crashed into a tree. He slowed down to get a closer look and noticed it was a refrigerated cargo truck with its back doors wide open.

Sam could hear the engine running and debated stopping. Then he noticed the driver, mutilated and hanging out of the cab of the truck, and decided against it. Sam pushed his foot harder down onto the gas pedal, looking at the wreckage in the rear view mirror.

Is that the Roslun Global logo?!

No Place Like Home

5:18

Gee still checked her watch often, knowing that time had no meaning to them right now.

It doesn't matter if it's five in the morning or five at night...either way I have to protect us both.

Alice walked into the kitchen, bright and cheery. She put on a good act, but Gee knew better. The past couple days had been trying on the both of them. They had to be on alert at all times. Sure, Gee boarded the place up pretty well, but nobody was perfect and nothing was secure enough right now.

It has been almost a week since the sisters boarded themselves up in this house like rats waiting to die. Cell signal was out and the last call Gee made was to find out that their father was in the hospital; the shock of everything being too much for him to handle. Outside the safety of the house lay death – walking, chomping, vicious death. When Gee returned from college to visit her father, she did not realize she would be thrust into the center of a horror movie.

Instead of coming home to find a nice family dinner waiting for her, Gee ran home to find her family *being* a nice dinner. Every time she closed her eyes, visions of Josh's young and mutilated body swarmed in front of her. Gee was too late to hear his screams; and for that, she was thankful.

"The incident in a Seattle neighborhood seems to be an isolated one," the news report on a little, black and white television set atop an old style fridge, snapped Gee out of her thoughts, "and we are being told that it is well under control."

"Why do you even watch that crap anymore?" Alice broke her bright and cheery façade and took on a tone much more like her mother after catching Alice sneaking in late. "All they broadcast are damn lies anyways. Isolated? Under control? How is this isolated? Mom didn't infect the whole damn neighborhood!"

"Alice, you need to calm down. I don't know what happened, but if the government says it is under control, then they must have some sort of plan in place." Of course, this was a lie; and even though Gee did not expect her sister to believe her, it oddly made Gee feel just a little better saying it. "And if we are ever going to have a chance to get your arm healed, you need to keep your stress down."

Another lie...This time, Gee hoped Alice believed her.

"I know, I know. I'm sorry. I'm just so tired all the time, and realizing I'm up at five in the morning makes me even madder."

"Then go back to sleep."

"Back to sleep?! I barely slept as it is. Can you hear those things out there? Moaning all night long? It scares the shit outta me." Alice pulled her black hoodie tighter around her young body and glanced over both shoulders, as if making sure there were no monsters lurking in the shadows.

Gee did hear those things all night long... those *zombies*. Alice did not like to say the word and never really had; afraid that believing in them would make them real. Gee, being more realistic about what had been happening, had come to grips with what they were dealing with. It's out there; we have zombies.

"Things? They have a name – *ZOMBIES!* They're real and the sooner you grow up and just start saying the word, the better off you'll be!!"

Gee stormed out of the kitchen and sat in the living room. She knew she was wrong, and that she would have to apologize to Alice, but right now she just wanted to be alone...to scream...to jump up and down...but she was strong...she had to be.

For Alice.

"Roslun Global denies having anything to do with the Seattle outbreak, and the cause is still to be determined."

Alice in Zombieland

continued the anchorwoman's voice from atop the fridge.

"'Cause they haven't fixed anything yet!" Alice threw Gee's glass pipe across the room, breaking the pipe and almost knocking down the tiny television set from the fridge.

Gee rushed into the kitchen, worried that a zombie had broken through a window. When she found Alice sitting on the kitchen floor crying, she knew her baby sister was not under attack from the monsters outside. She was under attack from the ones from within. She walked over to Alice, noticing the pieces of her pipe all over the floor.

"I'm so sorry, Gee. I didn't mean for your pipe to break."

"No worries, lil' sis." Gee sat down next to Alice and wrapped her arm around her sister. "It's just a pipe. I think we have just few, slightly larger, problems to worry about right now."

They both chuckled at the exaggerated sarcasm in Gee's voice. It felt good to laugh. It happened far too rarely these days.

"Why don't we get this mess cleaned up, and then go rummage through the attic some more and see what else we can find." Gee knew this would bring a smile to Alice's face. She loved digging through the old couples' boxes and chests. She called it their *treasure hunt*.

After cleaning the glass up, Alice ran upstairs while Gee checked the doors and windows. With everything securely boarded up downstairs, she felt safe enough to go treasure hunting with Alice.

"Gee! Look what I found."

Gee barely ducked in time to avoid being hit by a copy of *The Complete Works of Edgar Allen Poe* as she climbed the ladder. "Sweet. Now I have something to read."

After digging around for a while, Gee noticed the sun coming through the windows and looked at her watch. It was pushing six-thirty. Normally she would be getting up and going to school, but not today. Now her morning routine consisted of checking all the windows in the house and looking for any signs of life besides themselves out there.

The neighborhood looked like a ghost town now. During outbreaks, people are told to stay inside until it is over, though you always have those people who consider themselves *hunters*; but even they were nowhere to be seen. With the duration of this outbreak so far, the girls just wanted to get out of danger and find normality again. The risk became too great when they realized this outbreak was more serious than they thought.

So inside they remained - hidden out of view of the undead on the other side of the walls. Just barely out of reach of the monsters that wanted only to consume their flesh. This hiding became second nature quickly, which was surprising. It had gotten to the point that as long as they kept themselves busy, the girls could almost forget why they were only using one candle at a time, and never near a window.

Daytime is the only chance Gee got to check for any signs of rescue outside. This hiding had turned her into Pavlov's dog. This was why she automatically walked to the attic window as soon as light broke through gaps in the boards, and started looking for signs of *anything* at all.

Just a couple of those things. We could make it if we ran.

"Gee," Alice's voice snapped Gee back from her escape plan. Alice had gotten up and was walking towards her sister, holding something in her hands. "Take a look at these."

Alice set down the photo albums she had found while Gee was looking for salvation. Gee started crying instantly. Inside were the photos of an elderly couple. They looked happy. Each photo dug a hole deeper into Gee's chest.

"Why are you crying?"

Alice looked up at Gee with those innocent, sixteen year old eyes again. Gee wondered how much longer before those teenage eyes are forced to grow old before their time.

"They were happy. Before they ended up in those chairs, they were happy."

Alice in Zombieland

"But you didn't know them. Why are you crying?"

Gee cried even harder at this. One minute Alice was fighting for her life; and the next she was a perfectly innocent child. *How can any of this be right?* Gee wondered to herself as she grabbed Alice and held her tightly to her chest. "I love you."

"I love you, too, but I can't breathe." Alice waved her hands through the air; signaling mock choking.

Gee chuckled and released Alice. "Don't think this lets you off the hook for breaking my pipe, though." Both girls giggled.

As the day progressed, the sisters kept digging and playing, using any excuse they could to not face the terrible situation they were now in. Gee knew they had to get out of this house, but she was not exactly sure how to accomplish that feat. She knew Alice and herself could make it past those things in the street, but what about the next street, and the street after that?

But Alice is running out of time.

With the sun about to set, Gee knew their time to escape was now.

"Alice, I need you to go back downstairs and pack up our stuff."

"Are we saved?" Alice asked.

"That's up to us. Now go. Please."

Alice obediently did as she was told. Gee ran into the elderly couple's bedroom tomb, which had been shut up and blocked since the girls' first night in the house. The putrid stench of death assaulted Gee's senses, causing her to retch uncontrollably. Once she was able to compose herself, she quickly grabbed the shotgun and searched for any ammunition.

What gun owner doesn't have boxes of ammo?! One shot. Perfect.

Alice finished gathering the last of the useful items as Gee walked into the living room, shotgun in hand. "What is that for?" Fear could be felt on every syllable of Alice's question. "I mean...Are we...Will there..."

"Just in case. Are you ready?"

"Yeah."

After checking for any zombie activity outside, Gee and Alice started taking boards off the front door. The tension was thick, and lingered heavy in the air. Both girls could feel it, and neither one liked it. As the last board came down, they looked at each other and steadied their nerves as best they could.

"Are you ready?" Gee asked Alice as she took her little sister's hand in her own.

Unable to speak, Alice just nodded. Gee kissed her sister's forehead and turned the knob. With the setting sun being far brighter than the boarded up house, both girls were instantly blinded. Slowly they inched out into the yard, allowing their eyes to adjust. Out of the yard, the girls ran past a couple zombies shambling in the street. They rounded a street corner and came across a small group of fresh zombies finishing a light meal of friendly, neighborhood mailman.

With the zombies distracted for the moment, the girls decided to sneak to the opposite side of the street, making sure to stay behind the feeding zombies. As the girls inched across the street, making sure not to alert the feeding ghouls to their presence, Gee could feel her heart beating harder inside her chest with every step.

"Fuck!"

Alice fell in the middle road screaming before she could stop herself. Blood was trickling from her leg, but it didn't appear too bad to Gee. The zombies turned, snarling at the fresh meals that have just wandered into their vicinity.

"Get up!" Gee grabbed Alice under the arms, attempting to lift her to her feet. "We have to run!"

The hungry zombies were closing in, moving faster than either girl had expected.

Must have something to do with how fresh they are.

Alice in Zombieland

"Let's get outta here." Gee yanked on Alice's arm again, but Alice still did not rise.

"I'm trying, but I hurt."

"It's not that bad." Gee glanced down at Alice's leg. "Barely even a scratch. Quit being a baby."

"Not my leg…My whole body…It hurts so bad, Gee."

With cold, grey eyes, Georgia Marie looked around. The situation was tight, and she knew it. There was no chance of carrying Alice forward, past the oncoming zombies to potential safety. They had no choice but to go back.

"Argh… Grrr…"

Gee whirled around just in time to see one of the zombies from around the corner scuffling up behind them. Quickly she charged at him, shotgun held high in the air. Her loud war cry could be heard for blocks as she brought the shotgun, barrel first, straight through the zombie's skull.

"Alice!" Gee was so intent on finishing off this one threat that she did not notice a one armed corpse creeping up on Alice until it was too late.

Gee raised the shotgun, but not knowing how to shoot, she decided against risking her sister's life. As she stood there, too far away to help her sister, Gee watched the dead man meander up behind Alice. Sniffing the air, he walked right next to her, but his interest appeared to wane since he quickly turned back towards Gee.

Confused, but grateful, Gee ran around the zombie. "Get up! You have to run through the pain. We have to get back to the house."

Alice got up, and ran as best she could. The pain made running full force hard, but she knew the alternative was a lot more painful. So, through the pain she ran, fleeing for her life.

The street in front of the abandoned house was clear. The girls got inside and started boarding the door back up, knowing this was going to be home for a little while longer. Alice collapsed on the ground; her pain obviously getting to her.

Gee knelt down and held her sister in her arms. Together they wept, rocking and holding each other.

I can't do it. If it comes to it, I can't do it.

Always and Forever

"I love you."

"I love you too, but right now we have to keep our heads." Sam saw panic in Heather's big brown eyes. He wished there was something he could do or say that would make things better for her. "Something bad is going on around here."

"What is it?" Heather asked.

"I'm not sure yet exactly, but I don't think this is a normal outbreak. What I do know is that we have to get out of here. If this outbreak spreads, Roslun Global will do *anything* to tie up all loose ends."

"Can't we just leave? Go to Canada or something?" Heather was not one to believe in the weird and freaky, but she knew her fiancée lived his life for this sort of thing.

Sam looked into those beautiful, brown eyes and knew the only thing that would make them happy again was *We will be Ok*, but he could not say those words. "Maybe."

The wind whipped through Heather's window. She was cold, but rolling up the window was not an option; the fresh air was the only thing keeping her dinner from ending up all over the dashboard. She glanced over her shoulder at the backseat before she could stop herself. Bits of Heather's best friend, Tasha, were still all over the seats, even with the blankets covering the mess.

"There was so much blood...there still is." Tears rolled down Heather's cheeks as she fought even harder to keep from puking.

Sam stole a sideways glance at her, feeling his own pain. *I just want to make it all better for her.*

With dogged determination, Sam kept the car rolling forward at a fast speed. He was determined to save Heather and himself, but he was unsure what his next move should be. Everything he had seen and read never prepared him for the reality of it all.

Sam had played out zombie outbreak scenarios in his head since he was a child. In these daydreams he was an impeccable shot, heroically fending off waves of the undead while protecting those he loved... and he always knew what to do. These daydreams left the realm of dreams nine years ago when William Lohman stepped forward, and since that day Sam's motto became that of the Boy Scouts: Always be prepared. Now he was beginning to realize that everything he had planned in his mind was bullshit and he and Heather may be royally screwed.

"Where are we going?" asked Heather.

"I don't know," Sam replied wearily, his tough guy, man-in-charge facade slipping. He had been dreading this question ever since leaving the gas station. Even though he saved Heather from that zombie and became her hero, Sam was afraid to think of what she would think of him if she knew just how shaken and lost he really was. Heather had always been way out of his league, but for some reason she had stuck with him. Sam was not about to let her regret it. "We need to find someplace safe...Somewhere away from Seattle and this outbreak."

"My parents."

Shocked, Sam asked, "What?"

"We can go to my parents' house. They live in Kennewick, that's only about four hours away."

"Do you remember what happened the only time I met your parents?!" Sam winced as he recalled that night.

"That was an exception." Heather replied defiantly, noticing his exaggerated wince.

"An exception?!" Sam raised his voice. It was not quite a yell, but it would surely have attracted any undead within a close radius, had they not been driving eighty miles an hour.

"Look you want somewhere away from Everett, right? Is two hundred miles enough distance? Plus we know my dad will protect us."

Alice in Zombieland

"Protect you, maybe... The last time I saw his gun, he wasn't really trying to protect me, if you remember correctly."

"Either way, he has guns and I'm his baby girl." Heather blurted out in a *discussion* ending tone, which Sam recognized very well.

"Fine, but if he threatens to shoot me again, I'm out. I'd rather deal with the undead over your crazy father."

Knowing the police would be at the gruesome gas station scene, he decided the back roads would be a better option for escape. There was little traffic on the roads this late, so they made it to the interstate quickly. Sam aimed the car toward I-5 south.

After an hour of driving in silence, Sam checked to make sure Heather was truly asleep. Once he was sure, he steered the car off the interstate and pulled into the first gas station he saw.

"How ya doin?" The clerk was a gas station attendant cliché, a pimple-faced teen with braces. He seemed nice enough, though, and Sam hoped he would be able to give decent directions.

"Not bad. I'm a lil' lost though. Trying to get to Kennewick."

"That's easy dude. All you have to do is pull out at our..."

Sam stopped hearing the teen's directions. A news report on the clerk's laptop caught his attention.

"The incident in a Seattle neighborhood seems to be an isolated one and we are being told that it is well under control. Government officials have assured us they have questioned Richard Roslun, who denies Roslun Global having anything to do with the Seattle outbreak, though the cause is still to be determined."

"Bullshit!" Sam screamed.

"Dude, if you don't like my directions, then don't ask!" The pimply faced teen replied, taken aback at Sam's sudden outburst.

After apologizing and listening to the directions again, Sam ran outside and jumped in the car. Tires squealed as the car tore out of the parking lot quickly..

Isolated incident? Roslun denied involvement?

Somewhere between the slamming of the car door and the squealing of the tires, Heather had drifted back into consciousness. She looked around, still dazed, and asked, "Why are you driving so fast?"

"Things are bigger than I thought. There must have been two outbreaks tonight... Or maybe just one big one." Sam added frantically, "Or maybe this is the Final Outbreak!"

"Honey, slow down. You aren't making any sense." Although still scared and feeling even sicker than before she fell asleep, Heather knew when Sam got going, she had to be the voice of reason. "What happened?"

Sam took a deep breath to steady his nerves and collected his thoughts. He started again, speaking more slowly this time. "I stopped at a gas station to ask for directions."

"You asked for directions?" Heather chortled.

"Yeah, 'cause that's helping right now." Sam glanced at Heather and back to the road.

Heather hung her head and replied, "Sorry."

"Anyway, so as the guy is giving me directions, I see this news report come up on his laptop."

"He was able to have his laptop at work? Lucky."

"Baby. Focus." Sam paused and refocused himself. The anxiety was bubbling inside him again and threatened to take over. "So this reporter said there was an isolated outbreak, but now it's under control."

"So we're safe? We can go back home. What's the problem?"

"The problem is that it wasn't in Everett."

Puzzled, Heather sat up straighter. "Then where was it?"

"Seattle."

Alice in Zombieland

"How could that be?"

"Multiple outbreaks. I don't know how, though. It is even more important that we get out of here now."

Down the interstate they traveled. As the miles wore on, the sun crept over the horizon in front of them. There was no talk of zombies or Roslun on the radio – or in the car. From the outside, Sam and Heather's exodus appeared as nothing more than a leisurely drive. They could have simply been a young couple, in love and driving through the mountains.

The scene which played out inside Sam's head was a much different one. Zombies and theories swam around his mind. How could there be two outbreaks? Sam had only seen three zombies. Did that actually qualify as an outbreak?

"Ahhhh!"

Sam didn't even have a chance to formulate answers to these questions before Heather's scream cracked him back into reality. While his mind had been chasing down answers, a man wandered out into the road.

With a loud screech, the car began to skid to a halt. The car had not even fully stopped when Sam realized the man was not alive. By the time the car had stopped, the zombie had already changed direction and was making his way toward them. Sam shifted into gear and slammed on the gas. The car lurched forward suddenly. He managed to maneuver the car around the zombie, and for a moment it all looked like smooth sailing to Sam.

His short-lived relief turned into horror as the car slammed into a cement median. Sam jumped out and immediately saw a flat tire on the driver's side of the car. He scanned the rest of the car. It appeared to be in working order. Car assessed, Sam swiveled his head around to locate the zombie. It was about twenty yards away, but steadily moving towards the car. Sam knew what he had to do.

"Heather, I need to change the tire." Sam said as he reached in through the open window and jerked the keys from the ignition. He ran around to the trunk and popped it open. Luckily, Tasha kept a jack and a spare there.

Heather hung her head out the window and yelled back at Sam, "What do you want me to do?"

"Stay in the car and roll the window up. If that thing gets too close, I'll shoot it between the damn eyes."

I have time, but I gotta do this quick. With the speed and precision of a NASCAR pit crew, Sam jacked the car up and pulled the flat off. He could hear the moan from the zombie getting louder. He knew there was not much time left. *Gotta go, gotta go.*

As he reached over to grab the spare tire he pulled from the trunk, Sam caught sight of the zombie on the other side of the car. It had reached Heather's window now and was scrabbling at the glass with its dingy fingernails. Without even thinking, Sam pulled out his pistol and took aim.

Click.

"Shit!"

Click. Click. Click.

I have to protect Heather somehow.

Sam threw the gun to the ground and tackled the zombie. He was running on pure adrenaline and instinct at this point.

The zombie hit the ground like a sack of potatoes, and seemed almost confused for the slightest of moments. Sam leapt to his feet, but he wasn't quite fast enough. The zombie managed to grab at Sam's foot before he could reach the car.

"Sam! I'm coming."

Sam looked up from the ground and screamed, "No! Stay in the car!" But his screams were too late. Heather was already out of the car and charging at the rising zombie. She scooped up the discarded revolver mid-stride, and brought the butt down hard on the back of his head, causing him to fall back to the ground.

"Quick, run!" Heather grabbed Sam's arm and pulled him to the car. "Get the tire on, Baby, hurry."

Sam looked at the zombie, which was struggling to get

on its feet. He shoved the donut spare onto the wheel hub.
I can make it!
In his haste he fumbled the lug nuts, dropping them to the ground like a shower of fat chrome raindrops.
"Fuck me!"
"Sam, hurry." Heather hoped into the passenger seat. The zombie had begun to close in on the car, again focused on Heather's screaming.

Sam swiped up the lug nuts he could easily reach, but there weren't enough. A twinkling spear of bright morning sunlight glinting off of chrome caught his eye. The last nut was just under the car. As he reached for the lug nut, he heard the scream. It wasn't the scream of a woman fighting for her life, but more the dreadful scream of a life being taken.

"Heather!"

Sam jumped to his feet. As his head got above the roof line, he saw the car door wide open. The zombie had ripped a chunk of Heather's shoulder out. Sam screamed; it was a guttural, primal sound that hearkened back to when humans first encountered large predators. Heather's body fell to the ground with the zombie hunkering down over it. The monster stopped feasting on her flesh when he heard Sam's cry. It looked at Sam with dead eyes, a chunk of Heather hanging from its bloody maw.

"You son of a bitch! I'll fuckin' kill you!" Before the zombie had time to make its dead legs move, Sam was on top of him. He bashed the zombie's head in with the handle of the jack, its chrome skin glistening in the sun until it was covered in too much gore to reflect the sun's rays. "I was trying to save us...to save her." Blood splattered on Sam with every swing of the handle. It mixed with the hot tears that streamed down his face. "I was so close. Why?!"

Sam continued to beat on the bloody pulp until there was nothing left of the zombie's head. After ten minutes he finally slumped to the ground; his energy exhausted, his shoulders and arms turned to jelly. He stared at the grotesque mess in front of him, not really seeing it. His eyes focused on nothing, until another sound got his attention.

It was coming from the other side of him. Sam forced his weary head to rotate in the direction of the sound. The muscles in his neck protested, creaking like rusty hinges as they turned his skull.

She's moving. It can't be true.

The thought registered in his mind, but he could not make sense of it right away. Heather slowly stood. Blood dripped from the spot where her throat used to be. She surveyed the world with her new, dead eyes.

"No! Please God, no!" Sam cried.

Heather cast those bleary eyes, once so full of joy and life on Sam. He looked back into those same eyes. No signs of life remained, but he could still see his one true love. All the memories they had ever shared ran through his mind; all the love they had made, all the plans for the future they had discussed. The joy... The pain... And now, the end.

As Heather shuffled towards Sam, he gently pushed her back. With every advance she made, the urgency of her hunger became more apparent. Each gurgled attempt at a moan was like a dagger in Sam's heart. When he could finally take no more, he raised the jack handle high into the air. Using both hands, he brought the sharp end down, piercing her skull.

A whisper, so full of love and sorrow, "I love you...always and forever."

Taken

A muffled "thump" and a loud crash pierced the previously undisturbed night air. The sounds of boots scuffling and tense shouts filled the darkness.

"Clear."

"Clear."

"Clear."

Seconds later another crash was heard, this one louder and closer.

"Clear."

Two girls lay huddled on a dirty, wooden floor in an abandoned house. The former occupants of the house lay upstairs – dead at their own hands. The two girls held each other in the dark as they slept. They'd had a long day and were dead to sounds outside. For the first time in a long time, their sleep was restful and dreamless.

Crash.

Even louder and closer. Still the two girls lay in their deep sleep, unaware of the noise that approached.

"Clear."

CRASH. The front door of the abandoned house swung open hard.

"Get up! Right now. Both of you."

Gee bolted upright, throwing one arm around Alice. She felt for the shotgun on the floor next to their pallet of blankets. Before her hand could find it, she was blinded by an intense white light. Rough hands grabbed at her from all sides. Dazed by the light and the sudden activity, Gee tried to fight back. Tried to protect her little sister.

"Let me go!" Gee struggled with a large man who had lifted her by the arm.

The large man simply replied, "Do not fight us. We will win."

"I don't know who the hell you are, but we are obviously not zombies." Gee continued fighting against the heavy hand that held her arm.

Unable to stir as quickly as Gee, and with her head still swimming with grogginess, Alice was yanked off the floor by another large man. The pain in her arm was wide awake, though, and it reported in sharply, setting her entire arm on fire. Her rough handling aggravated the injury even more, but the old flannel shirt she had slept in still covered it from sight.

"I said don't fight us. I don't want to have to hurt a little girl, but I will." Gee's captor gave her a rough shake, showing he meant business.

"I may be little, but you don't know what you're dealing with." Gee's eyes suddenly shifted from her normal watery blue to a steely grey. "We just want to go home. Aren't you here to rescue us?"

"We are here to clean up the area."

"Clean up the area? What does that mean?" Gee's eyes had begun to adjust to the light being cast by handheld spotlights. "You guys don't look like janitors to me."

The men that had so rudely interrupted the sisters' sleep definitely did not look like janitors. The smallest of the five men was still over six feet tall and weighed more than Gee and Alice combined. The men dressed in matching black uniforms. They appeared to be military uniforms, but there were no insignia or rank indicators on their outfits. Not a single mop or bucket, not even a sponge, could be seen between the five of them. Instead each man was carrying an automatic rifle, with a small arsenal of other weapons and high-tech gear attached to various body parts. Definitely not janitors.

"Look. Just do what we say and you will go home." The man speaking stood in the front doorway. He was a mountain of a man, around 6"6" and broad-chested.

"Georgia!"

Gee twisted in her captor's grasp just enough to see Alice being dragged to the front door.

"Sir, we have something here." A seam from Alice's faded flannel had unraveled during the struggle. The scratch her mother had given her was laid out for all to see in the harsh light of the spotlights. It was an angry red weal, with tendrils of green and black snaking away from it both up and down Alice's arm.

The Mountain Man in the doorway grabbed her arm. Alice flailed her good arm wildly in an attempt to scratch the man's face with her nails. With one motion he grabbed her good arm and bent it behind her back in a text book example of a hammer lock.

"No!" Gee shouted, and twisted free of the man's grip. She bounded to the Mountain Man holding Alice and jumped on his back; but before she could strike her sister's captor, the giant nailed the back of her skull with the butt of his rifle. With seemingly no effort, he caught her in one thickly-muscled arm and lowered her less-than-gently to the floor.

"This one is infected, Sir." A soldier had bent down to examine the discarded Alice. "Her arm is half gone already."

"She's coming with us." The Mountain Man turned and left the house with his goons close behind.

Alice screamed and struggled, louder and stronger than she had before. Gee could almost hear her in the swirling blackness and concentrated on the sound. The blackness slowly faded into a foggy gray and she struggled to stand up. She must protect Alice; she swore she would keep her safe. With everyone dead and their hospitalized, Alice was the only family Gee had left.

Slowly, Gee stirred and began to rise to her feet. In the doorway, the Mountain Man returned and was watching the scene unfold with respect. The blow he gave her should have kept her down for hours.

As she stood up tall, Gee tried to speak; but before she could, he rectified his prior mistake with a walloping backhand. The young girl was sent flying across the room and landed crumpled in a pile against the wall under a large window. Her body was down for the count, but just before Gee's mind was pulled back under the roiling blackness, she was able to see Alice through the front door.

A man had Alice in his arms and she was fighting. She was fighting hard, but it was not enough as the man pulled out a syringe and plunged into Alice's neck. Her body went limp and she was carried into the dark night.

My little sister is gone.

This was the last thought Georgia Marie had before the blackness took her.

Loves Avenger

Sam sat in his favorite gamer bar, AFK Tavern, and just...sat.

It seemed like an eternity to Sam, but still he just sat. He had ordered a Mana Potion, but it sat there, too. How could he have murdered her like that? Heather was the love of his life. The only woman he had ever imagined himself walking down that Star Trek wedding aisle with...

And now she was lying in a ditch somewhere, dead and probably cold by now. Sam had pulled her down away from the road; he couldn't just leave her exposed on the shoulder of the road, could he? Either way, the fact remained that Sam Ashe had killed his fiancée in cold blood.

Well, truth be told, it was not exactly in cold blood. Heather had become one of *them* – one of those horrible abominations that staggered out of Sam's pop culture obsessions and into the reality of his everyday life nine years ago. Sam tried to save her. They were on their way. But now...

"Hey, Sam, you ok?" A fellow gamer noticed Sam just sitting at the bar by himself, an uncommon sight. "Dude, you're always in the middle of a game or a convo or something. What's up?"

"Nothing." Sam's voice was barely audible except to those with four legs and tail.

"What? Try opening your mouth this time. Ha." The gamer started chuckling and gave Sam a hearty slap on the back.

"I said nothing! Try opening your ears next time!" Sam was on his feet and screaming, the veins in his neck and forehead looking like they were about to burst and spray blood all over the bar.

"Dude, I just wanted to make sure you were alright. Don't bite my head off."

The gamer walked away and Sam sat back down. Out of the corner of his eye he saw the cute girl behind the bar coming toward him. She didn't look happy, but she also looked a bit concerned.

"Alison, I know. I'm sorry. I don't know what got into me." Sam knew exactly what had gotten into him, but he didn't want to re-hash it with Alison right now.

"It's ok, Sam. I'm more worried about you. And where's…"

Luckily Sam had quit paying attention to anything Alison was saying. Someone's laptop down the bar had captured his attention. It was a news report and it reminded Sam of the Roslun Global truck he had seen when he and Heather had first left town; right after he had put two bullets in his girlfriend's best friend…

Sam shook his head, clearing the grisly memory from it. "Hey, sorry, but can you turn the sound up please?"

"Wha…Yeah, sure."

"That's right. There have been reports of yet another outbreak tonight. Earlier we brought you reports that the Seattle outbreak had been an isolated incident, but now we have had reports about another outbreak in the Everett area."

Just as I thought… A second Roslun outbreak.

"Roslun Global has already begun denying any involvement in this second outbreak."

Sam had heard enough. He turned from the laptop and bolted for the door.

"Sam! Hey, you OK?" Alison's honey smooth voice conveyed the genuine concern she had for him.

"I am now that I know what to do." Sam flashed his best hero's grin, but Bruce Campbell he was not. Alison thought Sam was on his way to the hospital after seeing that grin. She suddenly feared he had somehow gotten food poisoning, and though he hadn't eaten anything at the bar, she ran to the kitchen.

Sam rushed out to Tasha's Ford Escort and turned the engine over. It had been almost a full day since he first saw

Alice in Zombieland

Dirty-leg Dragger in the alley by his apartment, and he knew he couldn't keep Tasha's car. The police had probably identified Tasha's body, and may have had an all-points bulletin out on her car. Besides, it wasn't his, and it just wasn't his style.

Sam drove back to the apartment he once shared with the only woman he had ever loved. He swung by the apartment before he went to AFK Tavern, but he could not bring himself to go inside. He just stood on the steps and wept, key in hand.

This time was different. He had to go inside. There were supplies in there. More importantly, Heather was in there.

I will avenge Heather's death. I will carry on her memory.

Sam reached the apartment and walked up the steps. He took a deep breath and slowly stretched out his arm. As his hand crept closer to the knob, he was surprised to find that he was not so much sad as he was scared. But scared of what, he could not imagine.

Heather's dead. True story. I killed her myself.

His hand reached the knob and hovered just above it.

What could possibly be inside this apartment that would scare me?

With his mind made up to go inside, he twisted the knob. The heavy wooden door slowly opened. Sam stepped inside and looked around. He saw nothing out of the ordinary, but after the past twenty-four hours, ordinary was a relative term.

He grabbed the first weapon his hands came across. Unfortunately it was nothing more than Heather's curling iron. He looked at the curling iron and began to complain to himself about Heather's stuff always lying around. A pang of sorrow shot through his chest. If she were there at that moment, Sam swore would never complain about her anymore. But she wasn't.

Never again would Heather walk through the front door after a long day at work, looking exhausted until she laid eyes on Sam and flashed that dazzling smile. She would never again stroll down the hall from the bedroom, wearing only Sam's Sublime t-shirt and that smile. Sam didn't want to cry anymore, but he couldn't help it. The sense of loneliness was overwhelming. He knew there was a reason he had come back to this place, and he did his best to pull himself together. If Roslun knows that I pieced it together, maybe they sent somebody here.

A loud crash from the bedroom pulled Sam out of his thoughts. He nearly leapt out of his skin and dropped his mighty curling iron with a clatter. He rushed to the bedroom, ready to tackle anyone that was in there. He shot through the open doorway at full-tilt, but no one was there. There were drawers thrown all over the room. Somebody was looking for something, but what?

Sam quickly rummaged through the stuff thrown around the room, hoping whoever had been there left a clue behind. There was not much time, so after realizing that the intruder had either found what he was looking for, or there was nothing to find in the first place, Sam turned on the living room television and started to pack. The television worked like white noise for Sam, helping to keep him calm in a world gone to hell.

"The recent outbreaks have begun to make some people wonder if allowing Roslun Global to continue with their experiments is safe, let alone ethical."

Sam listened as the news anchors went back and forth on the hot button topic of the moment as he gathered up supplies for his mission. He had retrieved his gun before he left Heather's body but it was empty, so he grabbed the rest of the bullets he had purchased with the gun. There were only twenty left in the box. He reloaded his pistol with five more shots of .357 magnum hollow points. The fifteen remaining bullets he shook from the plastic holder and into his pocket.

The LED flashlight he kept in the bedside table, the extra

Alice in Zombieland

cell phone battery, the laptop he had shared with Heather, and some batteries were the next priorities for him. If he was going to be out there alone, he did not want to be completely cut off from what was happening.

"Dianne, this should not even be up for debate." droned on a man in a plain, brown suit on the television. "Scientific advancements come with a price. I agree they could tighten laws and security on Roslun Global, but what the company is doing will save billions of people in the long run."

Sam knew driving around in Tasha's car was getting riskier by the minute, but he had left his moped at her house. He would have to go there and switch vehicles. With his bag packed, he rushed out of the apartment, forgetting to turn the television off. The newscast in his living room continued as he sped off down the street.

"In other news, there has been a rash of thefts around Everett tonight...of women's underwear. It seems a man is breaking into homes, rummaging through women's bedrooms, and stealing their underwear."

Sam pulled up in front of Tasha's house and saw his baby blue moped sitting right where he left it. He killed the car engine, pulled his bag from the passenger seat, and hopped on his preferred chariot. Sam thrust his hand into his pocket and pulled out the spare key. As the engine buzzed to life, Sam realized he was missing one very important item. He walked up to the front door and tried the knob.

Shit. The door is locked. Now how the hell am I gonna get inside?

Sam skulked around Tasha's house, knowing no one was home since he had seen Tasha partially devoured by a zombie (and subsequently ventilated by the snub-nosed revolver that now rested in his waistband) just twenty four hours earlier. He tried window after window in the off chance that one would be unlocked. None of them were.

"Hey! What are you doing out there?" A nosey neighbor started screaming at Sam through a window, probably

Joshua Cook

thinking he was the panty thief she just heard about on the news. "I know exactly what you're doing, and I'm calling the police right now!"

"No... wait..." But it was too late. The nosey neighbor had already disappeared from the window and Sam knew she was serious. "What the hell is it with this neighborhood?! Fuck!"

Sam broke the window he had been trying to open and clambered inside. Frantically he searched for the one thing he needed before soldiering on.

Where is it?! I know I threw it down in here somewhere.

In the darkened house, a flash of orange caught his eye thanks to a bathroom nightlight.

"Jackpot!" Sam held his Skid-Lid helmet in the air triumphantly.

Sam picked up the missing piece of his puzzle. "Safety first, even during the apocalypse," he said aloud to no one. He buckled flame adorned helmet securely on his head and ran out the front door. Off in the distance he could hear sirens getting louder by the second. Sam buzzed off into the night, the flame decals winking against his black helmet as the police cars came screeching to a halt in front of Tasha's house.

The Subject

Smack.

"I am getting really tired of asking this."

"We told you everything we know." Two men in security uniforms were sitting in chairs in a large office. Each one of these chairs was equipped with thick, leather straps on each arm. These straps were getting a workout as both men struggled against the strong leather. Their once neat and tidy white shirts were disheveled and spattered with blood. "We don't know how the Everett outbreak happened. There was a crash. That's all we heard."

"That's all we heard." A man repeated as he walked around the two men. He was dressed in an expensive suit, dark blue, with a white, button down shirt. His jacket lay across a desk a few feet away. "Did you hear that, Jimmy? Apparently I pay these asshats to just sit around and wait until they hear something that pertains to the security of my god damned company!"

"Yeah, I heard them." A tall man with blond hair buzzed tightly to his head towered over the men strapped to their chairs. Jimmy Hawthorne also wore a dark suit, but his came from a lower tax bracket than the pacing man's suit. His thickly-calloused knuckles were badly bruised and dripping blood all over the hardwood floor.

"So what should we do about these so-called security men?" Richard Roslun continued circling the two men like a vulture circling its prey. Suddenly he stopped and raised a finger in front of his face, mimicking an idea occurring to him. "I got it. Let's send them downstairs."

"No, please, Mr. Roslun...Not that." The two men began crying and begging for their lives.

Richard Roslun smiled at the sight of the two men groveling in front of him. Their pain was his pleasure. He didn't enjoy their pain so much as he enjoyed having the power to cause it. "Get them out of my sight."

Obediently, Jimmy unstrapped the first man, who was so badly beaten he could barely stand. As Jimmy turned to unstrap the second man, a scream forced him back around. The first security guard was not only standing, but rushing at Richard Roslun. Before Jimmy could maneuver his nearly seven foot frame to stop him, the man was already at Roslun's feet.

With his arms wrapped tightly around Roslun's leg, he began pleading for his life. "Please, Sir! Please spare my life! I have a pregnant wife at home. She needs me. My baby needs me." The man's pain showed through the tears streaming down his face, but it was not physical pain that wracked him so much.

"You should've thought about that before you did a terrible job." Roslun gave the man a smile. "Jimmy, beat this moron before you take him downstairs." Roslun shoved the man to the floor and gave him a kick in the guts.

"This fuck was in my shit before you could stop him." Roslun raised a finger to Jimmy's face, even though he was over a foot shorter. "That will never happen again, do I make myself clear?"

Jimmy looked down at Roslun and nodded in agreement. The evil smile returned to Roslun's face as he watched Jimmy mercilessly beat the man. Jimmy made up for his earlier faux pas with his fists; Roslun's disappointment had been crystal clear and Jimmy had his own family to worry about.

Jimmy lifted the groveling man into the air with one meaty hand and launched him toward his cohort. Jimmy undid the rest of the second man's bindings. Roslun turned his back on the three of them and Jimmy knew that was his cue to finish the job. Both men could be heard screaming all the way to the elevator as Jimmy dragged them by tufts of their hair.

The past decade had not been kind to Richard Roslun.

Alice in Zombieland

His life was in shambles; his reputation slammed in the media daily. Roslun Global was teetering and the chips could fall either way. Then there was the animated corpse reintegration experimental subdivision – Zombie A.C.R.E.S. What started as the top secret Second Birth Project had become the openly public Zombie A.C.R.E.S. project. That openness brought with it extreme scrutiny, but it will soon be worth it.

Ever since Richard Roslun could remember, he had always been obsessed with the Second Birth project. He could remember his father coming home late at night, stressed and heading to the bottom of a Scotch bottle. Mom would try to calm him, and he would yell and bitch. Like a little girl, he would whine about all the shit he wasn't supposed to tell anyone, including Mom.

Richard had lost more and more respect for his father as time went on. The more hardened the junior Roslun would become, the more he grew to despise his father. When the decision was finally made that his father was too weak to fulfill his duties to the project, Richard sided with the others; putting an end to his father's life.

From the moment his father was murdered, Richard Roslun began living a different life. Roslun Global was all his, along with it great power. Roslun used this power, this ability to raise the dead with a single word, to take charge of the Second Birth Project. With a *real* leader at the reins, he knew there would be no stopping the project.

The leap to a fully functional housing division was his. Roslun knew the only way to turn the dead into the living, was to make them *live*. How else would the lab guys really be able to study these disgusting creatures? Roslun hated zombies almost as much as he loved power. He especially hated the smell. God how he hated the smell. That putrid odor infected you and every piece of clothing you have on. Roslun would just buy new clothes, but he could always hear the faint whisper of death emanating from his skin.

Once Zombie A.C.R.E.S. was built, Roslun thought

things would be easier, but he was mistaken. In a short five years, the project was plagued by numerous issues. Not only were the experiments harder to control than anticipated, but trying to keep everything quiet was costing Roslun a lot of time and money.

The information age was a great thing for mankind, though it did have its downfalls to the criminal enterprises of the world. With so many people able to access so much information, it was only a matter of time before the dots were connected. Roslun thought he had more time to fix things, but then William Lohman came along.

Now this damn experiment had gotten loose and managed to completely ruin everything. Well, almost everything. Zombie A.C.R.E.S. was not a dark secret that was only whispered about in dark corners and hallways under hushed breaths. His greatest achievement was out in the open.

The downside of the fame and notoriety Roslun enjoyed was the constant scrutiny of himself and Roslun Global. This microscopic poking was harsh when it came from the governments of the world, but the public at large seemed even more determined to get to the bottom of what went on in the heart of Roslun Global. Public scrutiny, inquisitions, and Senate hearings were bad business, no matter where you are from.

"Boss," Roslun's thoughts were interrupted by Jimmy's deep voice booming across the room, "they're taken care of. The lab guys say thank you."

That evil little grin broke across Roslun's face again. He just could not help it. "Good. The faster those lab geeks get their shit done, the sooner I can announce the Second Birth Serum to the world."

Whenever Roslun would go on his rants and tirades, Jimmy always thought he looked like an evil James Bond villain, set on taking over the world. Not in a highly intimidating way, though, but more like a villain from Woody Allen's *Casino Royale*.

Alice in Zombieland

"Soon the world will see what I am capable of. That Lohman bastard did me just as much of a favor as he hurt me! Take that, you fuck!" Roslun shook his fist at the air. "Isn't that right, Jimmy?"

"Yes, Sir." With Richard Roslun, Jimmy knew it was almost always better to agree with him.

"I think it is time to start stretching my arm out further into the world. With all the chaos and death going on in today's society, people are going to be dying to get their hands on the Second Birth Serum. It will be the most sought after drug ever created, and I want to control it all."

"We already have power with many corrupt officials around the globe..."

"*We*? Where did this *we* come from, Jimmy? Don't you ever forget who is in charge around here. The building doesn't have your name on it, does it?" Roslun laughed so loud at this that Jimmy had to fight his ever-growing urge to just knock his teeth down his throat. "Anyways..." Roslun was actually wiping tears from his eyes and trying to speak through the weakening hitches of laughter, "prepare the chopper. I'm bored here and I have shit to do."

Jimmy was already on the phone with the airfield before Roslun even turned to look out the huge windows of the control building, taking in his entire creation. The Second Birth Serum had been his life's dream, and soon the world would know to respect and fear the name Richard Roslun.

"Sir, it seems we have a situation."

"You always have a fucking situation! Why can't you handle it yourself?!"

Jimmy had to mentally calm the rage that was rising inside him. Even though every cell in his being wanted to rip the little Richard Roslun to meaty shreds, Jimmy held back. "Sir, you may want to handle this one on your own." Calming himself had become as instinctual as breathing whenever he had to deal with his boss. He had responsibilities and family to worry about, and Roslun paid very well. "The Seattle clean up team has reported in."

"Good for them. I didn't realize they wanted a fuckin' cookie after they actually earned all the money I throw at them!" Richard Roslun absent mindedly put his hand to his forehead, rubbing the throbbing vein that had taken residence there. If Roslun had been a poker player, this would have been his tell. Whenever the stress was to the point where he was going to blow, Roslun would grab his head and just sort of space out. Nobody really knew what he was thinking when he did that, but if it didn't work, hell couldn't hold a flame to his wrath.

Jimmy knew this particular idiosyncrasy very well, and seeing it right now shook Jimmy a little. He thought he was about to be the bearer of good news, but now with Roslun's attitude, Jimmy was unsure how this would go down. Taking a deep breath, Jimmy braced himself for the delivery, hoping the messenger didn't get killed in this case.

"It seems they have found a test subject..."

"So? Drop it off at the Blake Island facility and quit wasting my time. Seriously Jimmy, what the hell?!"

"This one is different, Sir. It's a girl. They say she looks to be sixteen or so. She was scratched, but her body seems to be metabolizing the infection at a slower rate than normal."

"Really now?" Roslun's attention piqued at this information, and his hand slowly dropped from his forehead. "There have only been a handful of experiments that would show slower signs of decay, but they were all too old to handle the drastic effects of past Second Birth Serum incarnations..." Roslun's verbalized thoughts trailed off while his internal ones kept going.

"That is why I suggested you may want to handle this one yourself. They have her sedated and are transporting her as we speak. Their chopper should be landing soon."

"Good. Tell the lab to be ready for her as soon as she lands. My public announcement awaits, and my prized experiment will be landing shortly. I must get ready."

Boy Meets Girl

The rain was coming down hard on Sam Ashe as he buzzed his way down the interstate. To be fair, it was not Sam that was doing the buzzing, rather his baby blue moped; which was pushed to the max. The speedometer hovered at the seventy five miles per hour mark. Sam had to get to Seattle quickly. There were answers there.

Answers? Is there even an acceptable answer to what happened to her?

Heather Young had been a beautiful, young woman. She was a brunette with curves in all the right places, but she had a style and attitude that was more geek than chic. Sam had never seen a woman pull off sexy librarian better than Heather. That's what first attracted Sam to her.

She had been standing behind the customer service counter at the Kohl's they both worked at. Sam just clocked out for lunch with a couple other freight guys. Employees had to walk past the customer service counter when they left the break room, and that was when he first laid eyes on her.

Sam was listening to Dan tell some overly-exaggerated story as they left the lunch room. One moment Sam was stuck listening to this mindless droning, and the next there was no Dan. There was no overly-exaggerated story about his bar conquests. There were only two people – Sam and Heather.

Having just transferred in from another store, Heather had not run into Sam yet. Though truth be told, it probably would not have done the poor sap an ounce of good anyway. Sam had never been much of an outgoing guy. For as long as he could remember, he was more of a loner than a social butterfly. It was ten times worse when it came to a beautiful woman...

And Heather was *beautiful*. Standing behind that customer service counter, Sam could only see her from the waist up. That gave him plenty to look at, though. Her white shirt was wrapped fittingly to her body. It was not tacky or whorishly tight, but the exact kind that a cute girl who frequented a comic shop would wear. It also allowed her to show off a couple of her best physical features, which Sam, being a man, took fond notice of.

Heather's brown hair was tied back in a ponytail, showing off the curves of her neck. Sam would always love the way she looked with her hair up, and it all hearkened back to that very first day. Then Sam and Heather's eyes met. Heather's eyes, being behind black, cat-eye framed glasses that only furthered the sexy librarian cause, were a beautiful brown. They took on an almost Medusa quality, paralyzing any man that would look into them.

All of this really spoke to Sam, but the final thing he noticed was the icing on the cake. Heather had this small smile parting her red lips, probably silently laughing at some joke inside her head as she filled out the morning paperwork. Most would consider a smile like that to be a sign of shyness, yet undeniably cute. Sam knew he had to see more of that smile.

Not right then, of course. Sam knew exactly how that would play out. He would walk up to her and try to start speaking, but the only sound that would come out would be a weird form of caveman grunting. Unable to control himself, his face would burn bright red and he would turn to run, only to find the rest of the Kohl's staff standing there staring at him. Sam Ashe, the complete loser who was out of his mind for even approaching the goddess at the customer service counter.

This was how it would go. Sam was sure of it, even though these situations never turned out as disastrous as they played out in his mind. *Better safe than sorry, though.* So Sam continued walking with his lunchtime friends.

In the weeks that followed, Heather and Sam never really spoke much to each other. They would exchange the typical "Hi" or "What's up?" and maybe even share a small conversation about the weather or how much they hated the management; but they would never actually talk. Day in and day out, Sam saw this beautiful woman, but would never let her know how he felt.

Sam had always been considered a nice guy. He would listen to anybody, give them the shirt off his back if they needed it, and just generally avoid making waves if he could help it. This was one of his most endearing features, and the one that helped him get closer to Heather.

Suddenly a horn blared and Sam was awash in light.

Sam was shaken from his thoughts by the unexpected horn blast and a set of bright headlights. Off in his own world, Sam had not noticed a Mini Cooper driven by a very large man trying to merge onto the interstate. Nevermind the fact that it was so late, or early, depending on a person's definition of the dark hours, and there were no other vehicles in sight; this large man in his small car felt he needed to merge right where the tiny baby blue moped was cruising along.

Slowing down to let the man merge into traffic (even though the highway was completely devoid of vehicles, save the two of them), Sam realized where he was and he steered toward the exit ramp. He was not completely familiar with the city, but he knew the quarantined neighborhood was somewhere in this area. Sam wished his moped had a radio so he could get news on the cleanup effort - or any kind of information for that matter.

He drove around the area looking for any sign of, well, anything really. It was two in the morning and there was not much going on, so any kind of activity was sure to stand out. The rain was tapering off, and Sam was glad for that; visibility had improved, and he could hear the night around him, not that there was anything to hear so far. The more he drove around, the more his mind wandered back to the reason he was there at all. Only one reason kept him slowly cruising through a neighborhood that may still have some lively remnants of a quickly-hushed zombie outbreak wandering around it.

Once they had started talking more, Heather and Sam became good work friends. They even managed to acquire cute little nicknames for each other – Ninja and Genius. Heather was Ninja since she had this uncanny way of sneaking up and startling Sam, though a lot of his startle was for her benefit. The whole time, Heather had no idea that Sam wanted to be more than friends. He had relegated himself to the perpetual friend zone, happy to see her almost every day, but dying inside because he wanted to see more of her.

Heather started talking to Mark, another co-worker, and they were getting very close. Sam knew the kind of guy this new friend of Heather's was, so he waited, knowing she would need her friend. As soon as Heather started having problems with Mark, Sam was right there to help. Still, Sam did nothing but care for and help Heather as a friend.

It had gotten to the point where Heather and Sam were texting almost constantly. They had become very good *friends*, and that was driving Sam crazy. He yearned for more, but just knew it would be a waste of time. She was too far out of his league, though.

Thanks to Sam's good friends at the Miller Brewing Company, he got over that hump one evening and began to tell Heather how he felt. It was not some great and momentous scene, as most scenes involving beer tend not to be; but while texting one night, he finally told Heather how he felt in an oddly, vowel-free and highly abridged way.

That led to a few days of Sam feeling weird and awkward, not that that was far from of the realm of normalcy for him on any given day. In the text world, things were a little different though. Through the faceless connection of cell phone texting, Heather and Sam talked about things and initiated the *pre-date*.

The *pre-date* was not Sam's term or his idea, and he had

Alice in Zombieland

always been unsure what it meant, exactly. "It's the date before the date," Heather would say whenever he asked about the meaning. Maybe it was the fact that all they were doing was hanging out at his place. Maybe it was a test before she allowed him into her world of beauty. Maybe his curiosity just amused her. The reason didn't matter, as that was the night Sam fell in love with Heather Young.

Once again Sam was yanked out of his daydream by a loud sound. Actually it was the sounds of shouts and the heavy rumble of diesel engines. He swiveled his head in an attempt to locate the origin of the sound, which seemed to be an awful lot of ruckus at that time of night; but in the dark stillness of the suburban streets, he could not pinpoint where the sound was coming from.

As Sam turned his head to look over his opposite shoulder, he saw the large black truck barreling down the road just before it could crush him. The baby blue moped hopped over the curb, sending the operator to the sidewalk, landing sorely on his back. Looking up, Sam saw he was not almost killed by one truck, but a group of three trucks that were traveling quickly, leaving about four feet between each bumper. All three were huge and black with tinted windows that made limousine windows look positively crystal-clear.

A bit cliché, isn't it? The irony of this thought occurred to Sam as he realized why he had not seen the trucks in the first place. *Where did they come from in such a hurry?*

Girl Meets Boy

A heap of a girl stirred on a living room floor. She rubbed the back of her head and felt wetness. *That explains the damn headache.* Gee rose to her feet, moving slowly with the pain, startling when a voice forced her back to the floor.

"Can you talk?" A man's voice emanated from the darkness in the empty house.

Gee quickly jumped to her feet, ignoring the pain she felt, and squinted into the darkness. "Who are you?" she asked, still peering around for any signs of movement.

"Oh, thank God! My name's Sam." Sam Ashe stepped from the shadows, his voice becoming more relaxed.

This sudden intrusion into her personal bubble startled Gee, who had been ferociously concentrating on the darkness. All apprehension was lost when Gee got a good look at the man behind the voice.

Sam Ashe stood in front of Gee, dripping water all over the hard wood floor. With her eyes more focused, Gee could make out the chair he had been sitting in, the floor soaked beneath it. A sliver of street light shone through a crack in the boarded up window and glistened in the puddle under the chair. *He must have been there awhile.* On his head sat a little, black biker helmet with flame decals, and parked next to the chair was a baby blue moped, water puddling on the floor around it as well. *If this guy was dangerous,* Gee thought as she looked Sam over once more, *it's only to himself.*

"What do you want?"

"I want answers, but you can't help me." Sadness hung on every word Sam spoke.

"How do you know?" Gee began brushing herself off.

"I've come a long way...I guess it won't hurt to tell somebody who I know will believe me." Sam returned to the chair, making a hearty squishing noise as he sat down. He motioned with his hand for Gee to sit in front of him on the floor, but instead she shot him a look and grabbed a folding chair from the other room.

"I killed Heather." Sam began.

"Who's Heather?" Gee scooted her chair back from Sam's, ever so slightly.

"My fiancée. She was bitten and I had no choice when she stood up..." Sam's eyes welled up as he told the story of what had gotten him to this point. "...So we left Tasha's and headed out of Everett..." With every sentence, Gee could hear Sam's sorrow growing deeper and darker. "...I'm just paying for the gas and then -"

Sam paused as he got to the attack. He had never stopped thinking about that moment, about the screams and the panic. *If only I had been out there,* he kept telling himself. *Maybe... Just maybe...*

Seeing his pain, Gee said, "I can piece the rest of that story together. Why are you in Seattle though?"

"Like I said, *answers*. I saw a news report that mentioned this outbreak and figured the two couldn't be a coincidence. So here I am." Sam stood and raised his arms in a *ta-da* sort of way. "I looked all over this area. Nothing." Sam wandered over to the boarded up window and looked mindlessly through a gap in the boards.

"What did you expect to find?" Gee walked up behind Sam and placed her hand gently on his shoulder.

"How the hell should I know?" Sam twisted away from Gee and punched the wall next to the window. "Anything would have been better, but I found nothing."

Puzzled, Gee asked, "What do you mean *nothing*?"

"Not one body, living or dead. I searched two blocks worth of houses in the past hour; just a bunch of looting, kicked in doors and broken windows." Sam was rubbing his hand, which told him how stupid it was to punch the wall by sending sharp pain up his arm.

Gee suddenly had a thought and darted from the living room. She ran upstairs and into the room where there had been two rotting corpses for weeks.

He's right. They cleaned it all. No writing on the wall, no murder suicide, no sign of zombies at all.

"What got into you?" Sam panted from behind Gee.

Gee brushed past him, and simply said, "Nothing."

Back downstairs it was Gee's turn to be the storyteller. She began with the attack on Josh and Alice, and how it had been Alice's mother doing the attacking. She continued on, telling him about Alice's bite and their attempted escape.

"They just walked right past her?" Sam asked from his wet chair.

"Yeah. I thought that was a little odd, too." Gee returned to the living room, gathering her supplies.

"Not odd really. The undead ignore their own kind. They want fresh meat, not dead meat."

"But Alice was," Gee stopped gathering her things and looked at Sam, fixing a steely gaze on him, "*is* very much alive."

"Yes, but the virus is still running through her veins. That means they *sensed* she was infected…" Sam stared off into space, contemplating this news, "That she was one of them."

"Alice is not one of those *things*." Gee looked around the room. "I'm set. Let's go."

"Let's go?" Sam hopped out of the wet chair, losing his footing on the slick wooden floor and toppling over.

"If you want answers, you aren't gonna find them around here or back in Everett." Gee helped Sam to his feet. "Truth be told, I can't save Alice alone." She looked him up and down. "And you can't get your answers alone."

Sam nodded his head in agreement. He hated to admit it, but even though he was fluent in all things zombie, acting on them in reality was a little different. Always a geek and never a jock, Sam was not in the best of shape. That was why he waited in the house that night. He knew he would need this girl's help when she woke up.

"Step one is finding my sister."

"Already ahead of you." Sam grabbed a bag that was sitting on the floor. "I found a laptop with some battery life and did a little digging." He opened the laptop to a single website and held it out to Gee.

"Roslun Global?"

"They are the only ones capable of a cleanup this large, and especially this quick." Sam swung open the curtains for dramatic effect, succeeding only in pulling them to the ground. "Besides, they have," Sam motioned air quotes with his fingers "a *secret facility* just off the coast."

"I knew there was something weird about them. I told Alice's mom –"

"Why would you tell her mom?" Sam dropped the curtain he was attempting to fix and turned on Gee. "Why would she care?"

"She worked at the Seattle office." Gee answered matter of factly.

"So her attack wasn't just a coincidence? That explains why they took your sister."

"Why?" Gee's demeanor was turning deadly serious as her blood began to boil. "Are you trying to say this was Alice's fault?"

"Not your sister's, her mom's…well, kinda." He backed away from Gee as he explained. "If she worked at the Seattle office and this outbreak originated there…Well you gotta see how that can't just be a coincidence."

"I don't see anything yet." Gee grabbed her bag of supplies and walked out the door. "Let's find this island… and my sister."

Blake Island

Nobody gets out of dis ya pit alive...

The whole room vibrated as metal music began blaring from a stereo.

Nobody gets out of dis ya pit alive...

"Skindred? Nice taste." Sam rolled off the couch he'd spent the night on and walked to the large bay window, looking out at the rising sun. "Definitely gets your ass movin' first thing."

"I like the older rock, not too old though." Gee walked out of a kitchen with two mugs, steam rising out of both. "I wish the power would have come back on half an hour ago. I could have just nuked the tea water then."

"Tea. Ha." Sam chuckled, grabbing one of the mugs from Gee. "I just want a nice cup of hot coffee. Last night was a long night."

"We're not at the grocery store, we're at my neighbor's house." Gee handed him one of the cups. "And the Edelstein's apparently did not drink coffee. I searched and found some caffeinated tea, so quit complaining."

Gee stood next to Sam, staring out at the still empty neighborhood. "Thanks for going back into my dad's place last night. I know it has been weeks, but after everything that happened, I just couldn't bring myself to do it."

"No worries. We needed some supplies and I was glad to be able to help." Trying to ease Gee's pain, Sam quickly added, "I didn't go back to the apartment for a couple days after Heather died. It's always going to be a rough thing"

"I don't think I can ever stay there again. And there is no way I can bring Alice back there. She must be traumatized."

Alice was dead. Sam was thinking it, but he would never say it. He can feel it. Why would they keep a little girl alive, an infected one at that? They wouldn't. No matter, though. The only way for Sam to find his answers, and get his revenge, was by going with Gee to save Alice.

"What about your dad? How's he handling everything?"

"Not well. He's in the hospital."

"Was he attacked, too?" Sam asked.

"No. He was out of town when it all happened. I tried to get a hold of him and when I finally did he already knew. Someone from the government told him what had happened and his mind just snapped. No one is sure when he is going to be out, so it's just Alice and me from now on." Gee finished her tea and grabbed the laptop. "Since the power's back on, we can charge this thing."

Sam chugged his tea in two gulps, trying his best to ignore the resulting burn in his throat. "I know the first place we can check. They wouldn't have taken her too far."

"But Roslun's Seattle facility is still under watch right now." Gee said.

Sam grabbed the laptop from the table and began typing. "Do you really think they would take her some place in the open?"

"In the open?"

"Yeah, where everybody can see. The Seattle area is very public right now. Remember that facility I told you about?" The laptop beeped a few times. "I am sure she was taken there. The only problem is that I don't know much about it. Luckily, I know someone who does."

"Who?" Gee walked around Sam so that she could see the laptop screen clearly.

As if hearing its cue, the computer beeped a few times and a video stream flicked on showing a man sitting at a desk in a home office. He was dressed casually in a polo shirt with sunglasses perched atop his brown hair. "Sam, you piece of shit, how are ya?"

"Pretty shitty actually, Will. You hear about the outbreaks over here?"

"Of course. Who's that?" The man motioned towards Gee, who was standing behind Sam.

Alice in Zombieland

"That's Georgia."

"Gee." She gave a little wave.

"Gee, this is Will. He has spent his entire life researching and digging into Roslun Global."

"Hey, watch who you tell." Will snapped through the computer screen.

"It's fine. She's cool. We were both caught up in those outbreaks. Heather was bit, man...So was Gee's sister."

"Don't tell me you couldn't do it. You know that once they are bitten they're –"

"Will, I know." Sam took a deep breath to calm himself before continuing. "I had to kill Heather. She came back and I didn't have a choice." A single tear rolled down Sam's cheek. He shook it off and continued, "But they took Gee's sister. That's why I contacted you."

"They? Are we talking about Roslun? Please tell me that we are." The man behind the desk actually seemed giddy with excitement.

"Yeah, but they took her to Blake Island."

"The state park? You didn't say that's where this secret facility is." Gee said.

"One and the same," Will replied. "Roslun is a very powerful man, with very powerful friends. He used those friends to set up experimental compounds around the country, kind of like precursors to Zombie A.C.R.E.S."

Will clicked around and a map popped onto Sam and Gee's laptop screen. It was a map of the United States, with small circles over what appeared to be empty land. One of those circles was directly over Blake Island, just off the coast of Washington.

"Each one of these circles represents a different Roslun Global compound. If the cleanup crew was ordered by Roslun, your sister would be taken to the nearest one."

Unlike Sam, Gee was not used to conspiracy theories and far out claims. "But how is this happening with a government facility right there?"

Both Sam and Will laughed before Sam finally answered. "State parks are one of the biggest scams in America. Some big, hot shot, like Roslun, pays off whoever he has to. That person then declares a state park or some other protected land. Mr. Hot Shot now has his own playground to do whatever he wants."

"Bullshit." Gee just could not wrap her head around what she was hearing.

"I know it's hard to believe, but right now we don't have any other choice."

Gee looked at Sam for a moment. This all sounded too far out to her. There was no way Will could know about all of Roslun's facilities. Then she thought about Alice. Sam was right. They didn't have a choice right now, so she had to just jump head first into crazy. "How are we going to get there?"

Will clicked a few times and a ferry schedule popped up. "There is no direct access to the island. The closest access is a ferry that travels within a few miles from it."

"Alright. Thanks for the help. Send me any more info you have on Blake Island. Gee and I need to make a plan." Sam shut the laptop and turned to Gee. "What are you thinking?"

Gee turned and paced the room. "You expect me to just hop onto a protected government island on the word of some geek?" Gee raised her hands and looked out the large bay window.

"Yes."

Just jump in head first, Gee. For Alice.

"Fine. Let's do it." Gee walked back to the table where Sam had been packing some weed into a psychedelic colored mushroom pipe.

"I'm glad you're coming with." Sam takes a hit of the pipe and exhales. "I know this seems like something out of a bad zombie story, but this may be the only chance we have."

Gee grabbed the pipe from Sam and took a hit. She stared at the colors of the glass pipe as she exhaled. "Alice is

Alice in Zombieland

the only family I really have. My mom died a long time ago and dad has never really been the same." She took another hit and held it in for a moment before exhaling. "When Alice was born, it gave my dad a new lease on life."

"I think I get it. Hurry up and finish that, we have to find your family."

Family Matters

"So how do you know all of this?" Gee asked the open laptop sitting on the table as she rushed past it. Sam and Gee have been sitting in her neighbor's house for two days now; gathering supplies and getting more information out of the man who wants Roslun destroyed more than anyone.

"Research." Will's voice replied from the laptop.

As usual, Will was dressed in a polo shirt; today's color of choice was forest green. He wore a white visor on his head, and a pair of sunglasses on top of that.

Gee did not care where the information came from, only that it was correct. The past two days spent hiding right next to her father's own house has been terrible for her. Sam went over anytime they needed something that may have been in there. Gee was informed that there were no bodies or signs of death, just a lot of broken stuff, but still the thought of walking back into that house was unbearable for her. Even though the bodies of her stepbrother and stepmother were gone, the remnants of all that violence still remained. The patio door her mother crashed through would still be broken. The backyard would still be a disaster area. Alice would still be missing. Gee knew that someday she would have to go back to that house, but today was not that day.

"So you're sure all this info is right?" Sam walked into the large dining room carrying an armful of supplies. His arms had reached their holding capacity by the time he reached the wooden table. Sam gave a slight lunge forward, hoping to land most of the payload on the table, but failed miserably. Broken flashlights, crushed Twinkies, and miscellaneous canned goods spread out all over the floor around him. "Son of a bitch!"

"Whoa there." Gee walked over to Sam. For the first time, he noticed how her brown hair glowed in the sunlight as she crossed a large window. She rested her hand on Sam's shoulder and bent down, "If it makes you feel any better, most of this is useless to us anyways." She picked up a can of Spam, "We aren't camping. This has to be an in and out trip. Pack lightly."

"It doesn't make me feel any better." Sam grabbed some more cans and pouted off back into the kitchen, but not before stealing a backward glance at Gee in the sunlight.

Gee shook her head and continued packing her faded green bag. "*Shemp* there did have a good question before the crash..." She stopped packing and looked dead into Will's brown eyes. "This information is accurate, right?"

"It's as accurate as it can be. There may be some improvising on the island. This is not going to be a vacation." Will told Gee in his usual serious tone.

"Yeah, I'm aware of that." Gee went back to stuffing her backpack. "I will do anything to get Alice back."

"Me too."

Gee looked up to see Sam walking back into the dining room, an armful of Twinkies in tow. "I thought you were putting that stuff back?"

"I put the canned food back. I would never waste good munchies, though." Sam smiled a wide, toothy smile and shoved the yellow goodies into a SpongeBob backpack. The cartoon character was smiling at the world and dressed in a baseball uniform.

"Nice bag you have there." Will laughed from behind his desk.

"It was the only bag that didn't have any holes in it." Sam grumbled at the laptop.

"Grab one from another house." Will suggested.

Sam glanced at Gee before replying, "There are more important things to worry about than my bag." In a much chipper tone, he added, "Plus how awesome is getting baked and watching SpongeBob? I can deal with that." At that he zipped up the blue bag and walked it to the living room.

Alice in Zombieland

"Alright, Will. Looks like we have everything we need from you." Gee grabbed a water-proof map they found in the basement and opened it. "Roslun's compound is on the eastern side of the island. The ferry should pass closest to it right here." She tapped a different red circle on the map for every point she made. "But the question is how are we going to get from the ferry to the island?"

"I can't do everything for you. I'm sure you two bright kids can figure it out." Will chuckled, but continued on, "Remember, once you reach Blake Island, it should be smooth sailing until you reach the compound."

"That's good news at least." Gee finished packing her bag and carried it into the living room, passing Sam as he re-entered the dining room.

Sam leaned on the table, looking down at the laptop. "Alright, Will. Thanks for everything. I'd say we'll tell you what happens, but I'm sure you will already know."

"That is so true." Will and Sam shared a good laugh at this. "Good luck, guys," Will gave a fake salute as he signed off.

The screen went blank and Sam's gaze met Gee's as they both looked up. Without saying a word, they knew the time to leave had come. People in the neighborhood were slowly returning to their homes; well, the ones that were lucky enough to be alive were returning. Sam and Gee had bags packed and were armed with all the information they were going to get. There was no reason to wait around any longer.

They both grabbed their black hoodies and walked out the front door. Waiting in the front yard like a trusty steed was Sam's faithful, baby blue moped. Sam handed Gee the black, flamed helmet and straddled the bike. Once Gee was situated behind him, the baby blue moped sprung to life and the duo headed on down the street.

As Sam's trusty moped zoomed toward the ocean to board the ferry, a billboard caught Gee's eye. The billboard screamed fun and adventure aboard one of their tour boats, but that was not the part that grabbed Gee's eye. The destination did – Blake Island. She slapped Sam's shoulder, who got startled by the sudden and unexpected hit, and swerved before gaining control of the moped again. "Turn around."

Sam and Gee stood, staring up at the billboard for a Tillicum Village tour boat going directly to Blake Island. "Terrible idea." Sam turned and got back onto his trusty, baby blue steed. "Do you want to signal to Roslun that we are coming?"

"Huh?" Gee reluctantly put on the helmet and climbed back onto the scooter.

Sam sighed in exasperation. "Don't you think Roslun will have the tour boats monitored? He is experimenting with the walking dead over there. That is pretty hush-hush stuff, even after the Lohman interview."

"Won't he have the ferries monitored, as well?" Gee asked into the breezy forty mile an hour wind.

"Maybe, but it is more likely that a threat will come on a tour boat than to swim from a moving ferry."

"I guess...Wait a minute..." Gee paused to make sure she heard everything correctly, "Did you say swim from the ferry?"

"Yes, ma'am." Sam nodded. "I will explain when we stop, but the distance doesn't look too far on the map."

"You realize that maps are not actual distance, right? It is more than an *inch* to the shore."

"It's gonna be a swim, but it won't kill us."

The pair rode on through the tree lined scenery that made up the Seattle area. For a July afternoon, it was milder than usual. If it was not for the dire circumstances, this would be a perfect day to take it all in and relax. As they got closer to the ferry terminal at Fauntleroy, Sam pulled over at a rest area.

"We're almost there. I think we need to go over something." Sam sat on top of a weathered, picnic table and pulled out the map marked in red. "The ferry comes within a mile of Blake Island, according to this map." Sam pointed to a watery area on the map and Gee came in closer to read the legend. "A mile is a rough swim, but not impossible."

Gee ran her left hand through her helmet hair and looked off into the trees. "OK. Let's do it."

"Are you sure?" Sam asked.

Gee spun and back on the map. "Yes, I'm sure, but we can't take your baby then." Sam looked sideways at his moped, and then continued to listen. "We can leave it in the parking lot. It should be there for us when we get back."

"Unless somebody steals it, but who would do something like that?" Sam chuckled.

With one final check of their bags, they headed out for Fauntleroy Terminal. Once there, they parked Sam's baby blue chariot in the lot and boarded the ferry. They searched for a spot on the deck with minimal people and waited. The ferry had another fifteen minutes before it left the dock and almost another twenty minutes before they reached the point where they would jump.

"You don't talk much about you and Alice. Why?" Sam sipped on the hot coffee he'd picked up from a machine and took a seat beside Gee.

"We were never very close. My dad left my mom when I was very young, so I was jealous when he had his new little girl." Gee stood and leaned over the railing, looking deep into the water. "I know it was stupid, but he was my daddy. Not hers. As I got older, I knew it was dumb and outgrew those feelings of jealousy. Well, for the most part."

"So did you guys become closer as you got older?" Sam asked, looking into the blue water beside Gee.

"Not really. I always had my own things going on. Three years difference is a long time when you're young." Gee's voice took on a regretful tone as she continued, "I was in high school and now college. I'm almost twenty. There was no time for little kids. I always regretted not spending that time with her; not sharing that intimacy that all sisters naturally do." Gee's eyes began to water, but she managed to stop the tears before they came. Just when Gee thought she had her emotions under control, the motor revved up and the ferry lurched to life. The jerk of the ferry caused her watery eyes to overflow, and the inevitable downpour began.

"I love Alice so much." Gee cried in between deep sobs. "Why was I not a better sister? Maybe if I had come home earlier Alice would still be alive." The tears came on faster as Gee cried louder into the clean, ocean breeze. "And Josh. Oh my God, poor little Josh." Images of the gruesome scene where mother attacked child sprung into her head, causing the sobbing to take on a deeper, more mournful sound.

Sam could not help himself and began bawling along with her. "We'll get her. I promise you, we'll save her." He grabbed Gee and pulled her into his tight embrace.

The two stood on the deck of the ferry, sobbing and holding each other in the afternoon sunlight. After a few moments, they let each other go, and silently began to prepare their things. They both eyed the deck to make sure nobody was watching. With one final look into each other's eyes, Gee and Sam dove into the cold waters of the Puget Sound.

Alice in Zombieland

1

"Alice, what are you doing?!" The night air was calm, with a slight chill to it. As Gee screamed for her life, mist could be seen forming on every word. "Why are you doing this? It's me, your sister."

Mist could also be seen coming from her little sister's mouth. This was not from her breath, as there was no breath, but from the fresh meat within her mouth. Sixteen year old Alice has just recently taken to gnawing on her older sister's arm.

Gee pulled her left arm back and swung as hard as she could, landing a punch squarely on Alice's nose. The sound of crushing bone was heard as the force of Gee's hit shattered her little sister's nose.

"I am just so hungry, Gee. I...must...feed." Alice, looking pale and sickly, clumsily advanced on Gee. Blood was beginning to leak from her nose, but Alice never faltered in her advance.

"But why me?! You know better." Gee ran as fast as she could through the thick Washington forest, hoping to find any place to hide. Quick glances backward showed the dark lines of necrosis that had advanced even further along Alice's arms. Soon the black tentacles would be making their way to her neck, and then her brain.

With confusion and panic setting in deeper, Gee felt the ground suddenly slip away from her as she toppled into darkness. The slippery mud had caused her to lose footing and slip into a deep ditch. As soon as she regained her footing, she quickly realized that both of her legs were broken. With step after painful step, Gee continued her escape attempt while Alice quickly closed in.

"I'm sorry, Gee." Alice grabbed at her sister with a grey and blackened hand. Her hands were unable to catch hold, but sharp nails managed to tear at Gee's jugular. Instead of screams, blood was now escaping through her open mouth.

Alice continued her attack, unfazed by the shower of blood. She dropped to her knees, leaning over her tortured victim. As Alice tore a thick chunk of Gee's neck out, she is riddled with emotions. The hunger was growing ever stronger. Alice could feel it taking over her young body, but somewhere inside her was also a sense of sadness. She knew what she was doing was wrong, yet somehow it felt like it is the way things were meant to be now.

"NOOO!"

Alice jumped up screaming and took a bleary look around at her surroundings. The figures of five men could be made out; all dressed in black and strapped with weapons and high tech gear. These are the men that grabbed her, but where is Gee? As Alice's mind awoke, she realized she was inside a chopper.

What did that dream mean? Dream? Ha! That was a nightmare if I ever knew one.

"Where are you taking me?" She asked, but received no reply. "Where are you taking me?!" She repeated her inquiry, this time louder and with more force. Finally, one man did answer, with the butt of his rifle. Alice slipped back into the darkness of her subconscious and hoped there were no more nightmares... No more hunger.

2

Richard Roslun had been pacing the length of his lavish office on Blake Island for nearly an hour. He knew that at any time his new *subject* would arrive on the roof of the building.

This little brat will single handedly be the key to saving Roslun Global... And my power.

"Sir?" A large and muscular frame appeared in the doorway of Richard Roslun's office. "The chopper will be here in five minutes." Jimmy Hawthorne entered the office. "The landing pad is ready and Dr. Ito has assembled his crew."

"Good, but tell the doctor this one is mine."

Even though Richard Roslun and Dr. Taki Ito have a long and trusted history, Roslun wanted to ensure things went smoothly. Dr. Ito wanted to be the one to inject the latest version of the Second Birth Serum, but even the slightest slip up could signal the end of everything for Roslun.

That will not happen.

"Very well, Sir. I will inform the doctors to make sure the girl is prepped and ready."

Alice in Zombieland

As Roslun watched Jimmy leave his office, he thought of everything that had gotten him here. It all started with that asshole Lohman blowing the whistle on Roslun Global and the Zombie A.C.R.E.S. project. After that, there were accidental (and not so accidental) outbreaks across the nation; which set off floods of protests and bureaucratic bullshit that slowly chipped away at the value of Roslun Global stock. Then that stupid bitch left the Seattle office after she was bit and caused one of the largest outbreaks in current history. Though, this last one may be more of blessing in disguise.

It *was* the Seattle outbreak that brought this subject to Roslun, after all. Finally, he had someone who was young enough to survive the changes caused by the Second Birth Serum, but also had the rare ability to metabolize the zombie infection slowly. It was this ability to slowly metabolize the infection that was most important.

In order for Second Birth Serum to be able to take hold of the subject, they must first have been infected with the zombie virus. Second Birth Serum then came in and acted as a biological add-on to the zombie virus, using the original DNA to build a more evolved virus.

Second Birth Serum started its effect immediately, but the time it took to fully absorb into all organs was longer than the time it took for the zombie infection to kill those same organs. The doctors thought of this as the *X factor* that had caused previous incarnations to fail. Second Birth Serum had to reach vital organs and take hold before the infection, but this was not possible for most subjects. Through mass experimentation, Dr. Ito's team found there was a small section of the population that metabolized the infection at a slower rate. They also discovered that once injected with the Second Birth Serum, a quick and violent reaction resulted, similar to a heart attack, as the body and the serum fought for control. Most of the subjects died immediately, their bodies not virile enough to handle the sudden reaction.

That's where this new subject came in. A sixteen year old girl should have the capacity to handle the Second Birth Serum injection; and when that girl also had the ability to metabolize the zombie infection slow enough, a perfect storm of science and death would merge. Like the Phoenix, Richard Roslun would rise from the ashes to reclaim his perch atop the world.

As Richard Roslun was planning his victory speech, the appearance of lights off in the distance brought his mind back to reality. Knowing those lights must be the chopper, Roslun walked out of his office and headed for the elevators.

"The pilot has radioed in." Like an obedient dog, Jimmy was at the elevators waiting for Roslun. "It seems the girl had woken up, but she has been sedated again."

"They didn't hurt her, did they? I don't want any extra damage that may interfere with this test."

Jimmy knew the cleanup crew had forced Alice back into unconsciousness, but he was not about to reveal that bit of information at that moment. Richard Roslun took *kill the messenger* to a very realistic place, and Jimmy was not about to become the messenger.

The elevator doors opened and the two men stepped out onto a rooftop with a helipad set in the center; across the rooftop stood another elevator. The doors opened and three men in lab coats came out, one pushing a metal gurney.

"Be ready to unload the girl, sedate her, and rush her to the lab." Jimmy told one of the doctors. "The boss doesn't want to waste any time with this one." The wind picked up and Jimmy yelled to the group of doctors. "There's the chopper now. Get on your marks and be ready."

As the doctors got ready for the landing, Jimmy pulled his pistol and steadied his aim on the chopper. If anything went wrong he was prepared to do what he must. The subject may be a young girl, but she was also infected; and things had a way of going horribly wrong where the infected were involved.

There was no time to dwell on those things now, however. The chopper was almost on the ground and Jimmy needed a clear head if he was going to be able to focus. He checked to make sure the doctors were in their positions and that Roslun was a safe distance from them all.

The chopper touched down with a louder *thud* than normal, and before anyone could even register what was happening, a man jumped from the chopper. "She bit me!" The man screamed as he

Alice in Zombieland

ran from the chopper, holding onto his hand like a child with a precious toy. The doctors rushed to help the man who had fallen to the ground, but after a stern command from Roslun, they resumed their positions.

"Leave him for now! Your only job is to get the subject sedated and get her to the lab safely!" Roslun was screaming loudly by this time. The doctors had no problem hearing him over the noise of the chopper. "Jimmy, get in there and get this fixed!" Roslun motioned towards the chopper with a wave of his hand.

Jimmy started walking towards the chopper when Alice suddenly leapt out. The girl scurried under the chopper and around to the other side before Jimmy could fire off his first shot. Alice was running full speed when she reached the end of the roof. As she skidded to a stop, a sharp pain shot through her spine. She turned to see what had happened, but the world began to spin around her. Going weak in the legs, Alice fell to the ground. Once again, she slipped into the darkness that had become so familiar.

"Is she dead?!" Roslun asked as he rushed over.

"No, Sir. It was only a tranquilizer gun." Jimmy responded.

"Good." Roslun turned to the doctors. "Get her downstairs and prepped for me."

The doctors were already on the elevator and working on Alice when the men from the chopper helped the injured man to his feet. The group walked up to Roslun to report in, but he was not happy.

"How could you guys have let her almost escape?" Roslun was speaking loudly and vividly, his hands emphasizing his anger with each word. "I thought she was supposed to be sedated?" He turned and faced the open air, pondering his next move.

The men looked at each other for a moment before one man finally spoke up. "We thought she was sedated, Sir. Once the chopper was about to touch ground, she bit Roger." The man nodded towards the injured man holding his hand.

"She bit him?"

"Yes, Sir. On the hand. Doesn't look bad though."

"Let me see." Roslun signaled for the man to come to him. Like a good soldier, the man obeyed the order. Roslun looked at the bite mark on his hand. "You're right; normally this wouldn't be too bad."

Roslun grabbed the man by the wrist. With his other hand, Roslun pulled out a pen and stuck it into the open bite wound. Blood trickled out in red streams. Between the pain and the shock, the man was unprepared when Roslun shoved him and he landed hard on the rooftop.

The man looked up at Roslun, noticing he had a gun aimed at his head. "What are you doing?! You said it wasn't that bad!"

"I said *normally*, but this is not normal." There was a loud crack as Roslun's gun fired. The bullet flied through the air and found its mark, knocking the man backwards into a puddle of his own blood and skull bits.

3

"Oh, we can swim it!" Gee ran her hands through her wet, brown hair, pushing water out. "Why the hell did you think we could do that?!"

Sam and Gee walked onto the shore of Blake Island. Both were fully clothed and dripping wet. Sam surveyed the beach and incoming waves for signs of his bag. Gee fished hers out of the water, checked the water proof bags and walked off down the beach.

"Hey! I need my bag, too." Sam yelled after her.

"Then get it. I'm not stopping you." Gee continued walking down the beach. "If I stay around you one minute longer, I may have another damn zombie to deal with."

Sam spotted and retrieved his bag from the waves. Chasing after Gee, he yelled, "Look, I'm sorry. It looks easier in the movies and shit...But we made it, right?" A wide, fake smile spread across his face.

"Yeah, we made it, but barely. Let's count the ways you almost got us killed, shall we?" Gee returned, annoyance and anger entering her voice.

"No, let's not." Sam glumly answered.

"Oh, we shall and you are going to enjoy it!" Gee sat on a fallen tree and began rolling a joint. "First off, we could have been sucked under the damn ferry when we jumped off - sucked under

Alice in Zombieland

the damn thing!"

"Yeah, so there were a few things I didn't take into account." The jog to catch up had taken the wind out of Sam and he was panting to catch it again. The sea brought the smells of fresh air and blooming flowers into the deep breaths Sam took.

"Some things?!" Irritation stormed into Gee's usually calm voice. "What about the distance we had to swim, and I use that term loosely for some of us." She shot Sam a dirty look. "Did you ever take that into account? Or maybe the ocean current... That ever cross your mind?"

Gee finished rolling the joint and lit it. Sam, seeing his chance to speak, retorted, "I never said I was perfect. I am sorry the idea was stupid and could have gotten us killed, but the truth is, I am happy we did it! We are here and undetected. So while the method was a bit shaky, the end justified the means. Now, we can keep arguing or we can trudge into those woods and find a place to nap and dry out." As this last sentence left his lips, Sam stepped back a little, bracing for the oncoming outrage that never arrived.

Gee calmly took another hit and passed the joint to Sam. "You're right. We're here and that was the goal." Sam relaxed a bit as he took a hit. Gee got up off the log she was sitting on and headed towards the dark trees. "With the sun just about down, the animals are going to be getting hungry."

"Yes, ma'am." Sam grumbled under his breath. He gathered everything up and headed after her, arms full and joint in his mouth.

4

"Make sure the patient is sedated." An older man, evident from the weathered age lines on his face, wearing an open lab coat stepped into a stainless steel lined surgery room. Dr. Taki Ito had been the right hand man to Richard Roslun's twisted death experiments for years, coming under his employment during the Second Birth experiments. Having been a surgeon in violent and war torn countries his whole life, Dr. Ito was well suited to handle the atrocities performed under the orders of Richard Roslun. Dr. Ito led much of the research and administration involved in the evolution of the Second Birth Serum.

"Yes, Dr. Ito." Another doctor checked Alice's vitals and looked at readouts from the machines she was wired up to. "She is ready, Sir."

"Good. I will let Roslun know." Dr. Ito walked to the wall and picked up a phone. As he spoke, serious, brown eyes looked out from behind a surgical mask. "It's time."

5

"It's time."

Richard Roslun hung up the phone. That phrase - *It's time* – once again set off a turning point in the life of Richard Roslun. The last time he waited for the phone to ring, and heard that phrase, was the day his father was murdered... The day he murdered his father.

This time, instead of ending a life, that phrase signaled the beginning of a new life. The power of the heavens was within Roslun's grasp, and nothing could stop him now. He slammed the rest of his Scotch back and headed out of the office. "Come on, Jimmy."

"So this is it?" Jimmy couldn't help but be excited, no matter how much he hated himself for it. All of the death that had lead up to this point was unbearable to think about. The number of lives destroyed incalculable. But the moment was finally here.

"Yes, Jimmy. It's time."

Both men entered the elevator and rode it down to one of the lower floors. As they exited the elevator, they stepped into a room that resembled the control room of a television program. There were television screens set into walls, every one blank except for one. Banks of computer monitors were set along two walls. In the middle sat a large, metal table. Around it sat empty office chairs.

Beyond this room was another, much more sterile room, separated by a thick glass wall. Unlike the first room, this one resembled an expansive hospital room. Sterile steel covered almost every surface of this large room. In the middle sat a hospital bed and on that bed was Alice; her long, red hair draped around her head and spilling over the side of the bed. Machines with tiny computer

Alice in Zombieland

monitors surrounded her. Dr. Ito, along with his assistant, was busy taking readings off the various machines.

After scrubbing up, Roslun and Jimmy suited up and entered the second room. Dr. Ito handed Roslun a syringe filled with a green liquid. "This is the latest version of SBS."

"Let's get the show on the road then!" Roslun exclaimed as he grabbed the syringe. "Jimmy, are we ready?"

"Yes. Cameras rolling." He motioned to cameras mounted in the corner of the room. As with most megalomaniacs, Richard Roslun had a flair for the excessive. This time was no different.

"Good." Roslun stood next to the unconscious Alice.

"This is the dawning of a new era for mankind." Roslun began his speech for the cameras, raising his arms like a circus ringmaster. "With my Second Birth Serum, death will finally be an option, and not a definite. The subject in front of me bears what we know to be the prime traits for SBS to take hold and begin its miraculous transformation."

Roslun looked down at Alice. If one didn't know any better, they would have seen compassion in his eyes. Dr. Ito handed him an alcohol swab, and he tenderly wiped a small area on her shoulder. Roslun looked up at the camera and began speaking again. "In this syringe, I hold the key to eternal life." He thrust the syringe towards the camera. "The Second Birth Serum will allow people to choose when they want to die." *People with a lot of money.* "Or give you that last little bit of time with loved ones." He stuck the syringe into Alice's shoulder and slowly plunged the green liquid into her blood stream.

"We should begin to see momentarily wha-"

Suddenly, Alice's whole body shook violently on the bed. Roslun jumped back and watched as the shaking became worse. Every machine was beeping some kind of warning and Alice's bed was in danger of toppling over. Dr. Ito and his assistant rushed to her side, but were stopped by Roslun. "Wait."

"But she could die." Dr. Ito's assistant cried.

"She's dead already. Let's let this play out." Roslun's eyes went wide as he watched Alice's young body spasm, rocking the bed. Then, just as suddenly as it started, the shaking completely ceased. The machines all went quiet, except for one. Roslun finally allowed Dr. Ito and his assistant do their tests as that one machine carried on its long, steady tone.

Dr. Ito looked at Roslun. "She's gone."

"Now we wait. Watch her and report any and all activity to me." Roslun walked out of the room as Jimmy followed closely behind.

6

The sun was already rising by the time Gee and Sam began to stir. From their respective perches among the tree tops, Blake Island looked amazing. A small island just off the Washington coast, there was nothing but trees as far as the eye could see. Once on the ground, Gee pulled a map from her bag. "Will said the Roslun facility is around here." She pointed to an area almost six miles in. "The land gently slopes upward, making for a tough, though not impossible, hike. We should head out. We don't have time to waste."

"I know, dude, but I'm so damn hungry." Sam said, rubbing his growling belly.

As they finished packing up their supplies, Gee hurried into the woods. Sam eventually followed, and found her sitting on a log, enjoying a salad. "You brought a salad?" He asked.

"No, I *picked* a salad. Look around." Gee answered, gesturing to the wilderness around them.

Sam obliged, then pulled something out of his bag. "Look, I picked a Twinkie."

"Mine's healthier." Gee replied in a snarky tone.

"Mine's tastier." Sam stuck his tongue out, imitating a young child.

Gee shook her head. "Anyway, back to adult world here. I think we should be there by nightfall if we really truck it." Gee said as she stared off into the trees. "Will said it was close to the middle of the island."

They both travelled through the forest in silence. The terrain kept getting rougher, and even though Sam was sore and tiring out, he would not admit defeat. After a couple hours, Gee finally brought up stopping for a quick bite.

Alice in Zombieland

"You make it sound like we're just hitting a Burger King." Sam laughed as he sat down on an overturned tree. He reached into his bag and pulled out another Twinkie, offering it to Gee.

"No thanks, I have salad, remember?" Gee held up a couple leaves she had picked and began scouring for berries.

"I was thinking..." Sam took a bite of his lunch and continued, "Once we get closer, there is going to be a lot of security. We aren't exactly waltzing up to the Comcast Arena or anything."

"That's why we have guns." Gee continued to forage as she talked. "We discussed this. They want her for some reason, and are willing to do anything to keep her. We have to be willing to do anything to get her back."

"I know, but they are trained killers. You're a college kid and I play *Modern Warfare*. What chance do we stand in a fire fight with them?" Sam finished his Twinkie in two bites and opened a new one, shoving the wrapper back into his bag.

"It's not like we are going in there guns a-blazing like the Wild West or something. We are two people with a plan to sneak in. The guns are only if they detect us."

"Which I'm thinking is unlikely. The short time I have known Will, he has been the expert on all things Roslun." Sam said.

Gee sat on the fallen tree next to Sam. While she mixed and ground her salad in a little bowl, she told him, "We can sit here and worry about it, but somewhere in these trees is a little girl that needs our help." She put her hand on his shoulder and looked into his eyes. "I need your help, Sam. We have to save Alice."

Sam looked back into her eyes and simply nodded.

7

"Intruders have been detected on the island." A guard sitting at a bay of computer screens enlarged a video image, "Two people appear to have come ashore and are currently headed through the woods."

Jimmy stood in the middle of the small security room and looked over the guard's shoulder at the monitors. "Send someone to stop them. Roslun is not to be disturbed for any reason today."

Joshua Cook

8

Still tired, Richard Roslun woke up to a picture perfect day. Outside his window, the sun was shining bright in the sky, blazing a sheet of gold onto the surrounding water. The trees were gently swaying back and forth in the breeze; and even Roslun could imagine the birds singing in those gentle trees today. Nothing could bring him down.

Instead of flying home, he had stayed right here at Blake Island. It was not out of the ordinary for Roslun to have to stay one or more nights at one of his facilities. Each facility had special sleeping quarters designed for this purpose. These rooms were more along the lines of a penthouse, but for Roslun it may as well have been the Cabrini-Green projects . Once he completed his morning routine, he headed upstairs to check on the subject, "Any changes?"

Inside the monitoring section of Alice's room were Dr. Ito and his assistant. "Nothing yet," Dr. Ito replied, "Since she reanimated, she has just been lying there." Dr. Ito turned from the monitors and faced Roslun, "I did not want to run any tests without you being present. I know how important this is."

"Start the cameras." Roslun walked into the large hospital room.

9

The sunshine. That was what Alice missed the most. For hours now she has been lying in the dark, staring up at a blank ceiling. Her memory was akin to Swiss cheese, but she could remember bits and pieces of things.

She was unconscious.

Then there was a bright light and a lot of pain.

Then there was nothing.

Alice awoke in this room; alone and strapped to a bed by her arms and legs. She was unable to move at all. Then someone came into her room and said something that would have stopped her heart, had it still been beating.

"The girl has been dead for about three hours. Are we sure she

Alice in Zombieland

is coming back?"

That was the moment that Alice knew it was best for her to just lay there and keep quiet. She may be young, but she was not stupid. She knew what had happened to her. There was nothing alive inside of Alice anymore, and she knew this. Last week, she was just a high school kid, hanging out with her friends and shopping. Now she was a monster; a creature that was neither dead nor alive. People would periodically come in to check on one of the instruments or monitors, maybe even throw a glance in her direction, but none of them would come close to her.

Good thing was they would still talk. Alice has been able to pull in bits and pieces, but all those bits and pieces just raised even more questions. She knew Roslun Global had something to do with all of this, but how or why was still a mystery. She also knew she was different from other zombies. There was no explanation that told her this, she just knew it. That was her first clue – she *knew* things. Zombies aren't supposed to be able to think. They were mindless killing machines and nothing more. She also *missed* the sun. That can't be normal undead behavior either.

How can something dead have any feelings at all?

10

"Time to get up!" Richard Roslun walked into Alice's room yelling. "I know you are back and I know you can hear me. Do you think you're the first subject that we have brought back?" He couldn't stop himself from laughing as he walked up to Alice's bed. Their eyes met as Roslun looked down on her, "You don't look too scary. I'm going to have that gag taken out of your mouth so we can talk. Do you understand that?"

Alice nodded in agreement.

"Good." With one snap of his fingers, Roslun signaled for Dr. Ito's assistant to come in. The man removed the gag and exited back out of the room. "There. Now we can talk. Can you talk?"

"Yes." Alice barely recognized the voice that she heard. It was lower with a deep rasp to it, sounding more like a growl than the voice she remembered.

"Good, so you are better off than most of these animals. Your voice will come back soon." Roslun pulled a cart over from across the room. "You are going to be the specimen that puts me back on top of the world."

"Specimen?" Alice did not like the sound of that.

"Yeah, it's not like you're human or anything," Roslun let out a hearty laugh at the mere thought of this *experiment* thinking she was anything more. "You will never be human."

Alice hadn't thought about it that way. She realized she was not human, but the certainty of never being human again never really set in. This scared Alice – scared her more than anything ever had.

"If you are done entertaining me with your crazy thoughts, I really do have things to do," Another snap and the assistant returned and freed her wrists and legs. He did not run out afterwards. "Don't worry about her. I don't think she is going to be any trouble at all." The man reluctantly left the room, shooting Roslun one last look on the way out, as if to ask *Are you really sure?*

"Sit up." Roslun commanded and Alice obliged. "Good. There doesn't seem to be any trouble with your muscles. Do you hurt?"

Alice felt stiffness in her muscles, like she had been sleeping for days. There was some cracking and creaking from her bones as she moved, but there was no real pain. "No."

Roslun turned around to grab one of the stainless steel instruments from the cart; but before he could grab anything, Alice was on him like a wild animal, leaping from the hospital bed onto Roslun's back in one fluid motion. She grabbed at his face as he madly swung around, trying to shake her loose.

"I'm not just some specimen!" Alice screamed while pawing at Roslun's face. Little bits of skin and blood flew as each scratch landed.

"You little brat, get off me!" Roslun grabbed a hold of Alice's long, red hair and yanked with all his might, throwing the young girl hard onto the floor. "Get her strapped in... Tight!" Roslun stormed out past Dr. Ito, who had rushed in during the commotion. Roslun was holding a bloody towel to his face. "Get those tests done. Now!"

Alice in Zombieland

11

"Are we there yet?" Sam nagged Gee. It had been another two hours of uphill terrain and his legs were feeling numb. He wasn't sure how much more of this he could take.

"It's only been a couple hours. We should be getting close, but whining like a little kid isn't going to get us there any faster," Gee answered without so much as a glance back toward Sam.

"I know, but my legs are so sore they're almost numb." Sam stopped and rubbed his legs.

"Man up, cowgirl. I am seriously embarrassed for you." Gee said as she continued on through the woods.

CRACK!

A tree branch fell, narrowly missing Sam's head and knocking him to the ground. "What the hell was that?"

"I don't know." Gee squatted down next to Sam and tried to look around. "Stay down."

CRACK!

The tree trunk next to Sam's head exploded as a bullet narrowly missed Sam. "Forget getting down, I'm outta here."

Sam and Gee tore off through the trees, running as fast as their legs could take them. No matter how fast they ran, the loud *crack* of gunshots pursued them. With a little distance finally made between themselves and the gunshots, Sam and Gee ducked into a vine covered cave and hid.

"Be quiet." Gee poked her head through the vines a little and looked around. She didn't see anybody, but she could hear voices off in the distance, and they were getting closer with each passing second. Her heart pounded harder and harder inside her chest.

"Be quiet? Easy for you to say." Sam whispered in a very angry tone as he paced around their hiding place. "If they find us, they are going to kill us. This isn't paintball or something." Sam's voice started to get louder as he became more worked up.

"Sam, you need to stay quiet. I'm trying to listen." Gee couldn't hear the voices anymore.

"I am being quiet. It's not like they can hear me out there." Sam replied, getting louder as be became even more anxious, each word carrying a little further out into the woods

"I think I hear something. Shut up." Gee whispered, waving her hand behind her back.

"Shut up? How can I shut up when we are about to be murdered?" Sam asked the air loudly as he continued to pace the cave.

Gee turned towards Sam and sternly whispered, "If you shut up, we won't be murdered. But if you keep running your mouth like a scared little girl, you are going to get us both killed."

"Too late."

Gee reeled around to see a man pushing through the vines.

"Thank you for being a scared little girl." The man said and smiled at Sam. He searched them both, taking their guns and bags. "Who are you and why are you here?" The man asked as he led them out by gunpoint.

"We're here to save my sister." Gee spat out angrily, feeling the tip of his gun against her back.

"Your sister?" The man laughed. "And who might that be? We have quite a few guests staying with us."

The man continued to laugh at his own joke; so lost in that laughter that he didn't hear the sound of twigs snapping behind him. Suddenly a shot rang out and the man fell to his knees, grabbing at his chest. Blood poured from the behind his hand.

Sam and Gee looked around and saw a man standing near tree. He was a tall and muscular man, covered from head to toe in black stealth gear. "Go. You are running out of time." The man turned and ran off through the woods.

"You heard the man, run." Gee grabbed Sam's arm and they took off towards the facility.

12

"At least you weren't bit. This does not mean automatic death," Dr. Ito was cleaning the scratches on Roslun's face. "She was kept in a sterile environment and is newly dead. It is likely that the bacteria on her hands may not be as contaminated as those of a normal experiment."

"That's no consolation." Roslun pushed the doctor's hand aside, "Nobody is going to want a dead leader, so this stays between us."

Alice in Zombieland

"Not a word, of course." Dr. Ito packed up his supplies. "We do have more pressing matters at hand. We ran the tests on the girl and it appears she is functioning well above any of our predictions."

"So SBS is a success." Roslun said triumphantly.

"Not exactly, Richard. The girl still has all the functions she had when she was alive, but they are dying." The doctor continued calmly, knowing Roslun would need a simple explanation. "Everything that makes her human, the success you want to celebrate, is slowly dying - her ability to talk, think, everything. Eventually she will be exactly like the rest of those corpses down there."

"How long before it all shuts down?"

"There is no way of knowing. There are some experiments down there almost a year old, still able to talk and think. We have to monitor and continually track her condition."

"Keep her locked up with the other experiments so we can study her."

"Yes. Sir."

13

Alice looked around the room she had been thrown into. The hospital room had given way to solitary confinement. Instead of glass walls, she was surrounded by cold, grey steel and cement; in the middle of the ceiling hung one single 60 watt bulb, which stayed on constantly. That was it. When she was thrown in this hell hole, Alice was told by the guards – in not so kind tones – that since the experiments are dead, they have no need for the *luxuries* of the living. They were nice and threw in a folding chair with some outdated women's magazines, but the *luxuries* the living enjoy, like beds, showers, and toilets, were all absent.

The walls looked strong and thick, but voices continued to slip through all night long. Some of the voices were other *experiments* crying in a low, sad wail. Other voices were actually speaking words. These people were speaking to anyone willing to listen about the last memories they had. Tales of death and destruction invaded Alice's ears.

It was wet... The car slid... and then I woke up here...

Joshua Cook

There were other tales as well though, tales of love and of loss. Men and women were screaming for their families; begging for one last minute or one last hug. Wives cried out for their husbands while husbands cried out for their wives. Parents screamed for their children.

Mary... I love you, Mary... Daddy misses you so much...

The ones that really got to Alice were the children. She could not hear many of them, but the ones she heard were enough to stay with her forever. Most of them just cried. In between the sobs, words could be made out, things such as cancer and car accidents. It was a relief to know that Roslun wasn't out killing children for his experiments, but it was disturbing to Alice nonetheless.

One voice in a nearby cell stood out to Alice. It was the voice of a man. His voice did not stand out because of the story it told, or the condition of the voice, which was a close second only to Alice's. It stood out because it was only repeating two words over and over again. "I'm sorry."

Alice did not want to draw too much attention to herself, so she stayed quiet most of the time she was in her cell. After a while though, one question nagged at her. The more those words were repeated, the more Alice felt the need to ask.

Finally she asked, "What are you sorry for?" She waited, but heard no reply. She tried again, a little louder this time, "What are you sorry for?"

"Everything."

Intrigued, Alice asked, "Who are you?"

"Who I am doesn't matter anymore. I need to tell somebody." The man's voice replied.

"Tell somebody what?" Alice caught her voice getting louder and quickly hushed it down a bit. "What's wrong?"

"I work, well *worked*, for Roslun. The Seattle outbreak was no accident."

Alice's eyes got wide as this news made its way through the walls of the zombie prison. "What do you know about the Seattle outbreak?" She inched closer to the cold, grey wall, anxiously awaiting the reply.

"I worked at the Seattle office. There are secret floors beneath the lab, only a couple, though. That is where the final preparations

Alice in Zombieland

are made to SBS before it is brought here for final testing." The man began to explain.

"SBS?" Alice had heard the name during her stay here, but she hadn't been able to figure out what it meant.

"Second Birth Serum. That's the stuff they injected us with."

"What about Seattle? I was caught in that outbreak." Alice was having a hard time keeping her voice low. If this man knew something about what happened to her family, she had to find out.

"It's you?" The man's voice sounded surprised. "You are the one they just brought in from the coast?"

"Yeah. How did you know?" Feeling paranoid, Alice instinctively looked over her shoulder.

"You need to get out of here. It is not safe for you." Panic began to set into the stranger's voice. "You must find a way to escape."

"But how?" Alice stopped worrying about the volume of her voice, "I'm just a high school kid."

"You are more. My time is up." Suddenly Alice heard the sound of a cell door being opened. "Hurry. You must hurry."

There was a loud bang and then silence.

Alice listened closely, but heard nothing except the moans and wails of the other prisoners.

14

"There's the north wall." Gee pointed through the trees toward a tall cement wall. "According according to Will, there is a blind spot in the north eastern corner. The dense trees make it hard for the guards to see. We can sneak up to the wall without being noticed."

"And then scale a ten foot wall, with a flat face by the way, and run in to save your sister? Sounds like a great plan." Sam added, sarcastically.

"No you idiot. Were you not listening at all on the ferry?"

"Nope." Sam replied flatly.

"Very mature. Well listen now." Gee shook her head and pulled out the map marked with notes and scribbles. "Right here is where we need to be when the sun starts to set. There is a sewage tunnel underneath that runs out right there."

"Seriously? What is this, some cheesy action movie?" Sam laughed to himself as he imagined him in a wife beater, running through the jungle *Rambo*-style.

"If it was, I would have killed you already, now listen. Once we get in through the sewer tunnel, Will says it is only a little way until we reach the ladder that leads upstairs. Then we just have to head down a couple corridors and we are in the prison area." Gee stopped and looked at Sam. "Why would they keep people locked up here anyways?"

"Roslun will do anything to protect his power. If that means locking up a few lowly nobodies, then so be it." Sam answered.

"We have to hurry. The sun is about to set." Gee packed up the map and they set out through the trees. The ground was a little drier here, which made the trek a little easier and quicker than it had been so far. Within thirty minutes, they reached the north eastern corner.

Crouching low, they scoped out the surroundings. "Will was right. There is no way the guards can see this low from their perches on top of the wall." Sam tapped Gee on the shoulder and pointed to the left. In the darkness she could barely make out an opening in the wall. Slowly, they rose and made their way to the sewage tunnel.

"Man that stinks." Sam held his nose as they approached the tunnel. "And we have to walk through this mess? No thanks." He waved his hands in front of him in protest.

"That's fine. You can stay out here in the dark and wait for me." Gee suggested.

As if that was their cue, various animals began howling in the dark. Sam looked around, obviously scared, and said, "Nah, I can deal."

"That's what I thought. Come on."

15

"And where the hell were you?!" Jimmy Hawthorne walked into Richard Roslun's office and instantly got an earful. "I was attacked and you were nowhere to be found! What the fuck do I pay you

Alice in Zombieland

for?!"

Jimmy calmly replied, "I apologize, Sir. There was an urgent matter I had to take care of."

"Don't leave me to be attacked by another one of those animals again, or *you* will be the next experiment!" Roslun stormed past Jimmy and out of his office.

Jimmy followed close behind as they headed down the hall. "So how is the girl?"

Roslun stopped and turned so quickly Jimmy almost fell as he tried to stop. "She is the one that did this to me." Roslun pointed to his bandaged face. Jimmy could see blood leaking through the white bandages. "If I didn't need her so badly, I would beat the crap out of her myself."

A call came over Jimmy's radio as the two men entered the elevator. "The intruders are in the sewage tunnels." The voice informed them.

"Intruders? Why didn't I know about any intruders?" Roslun looked at Jimmy, waiting for an answer.

"It's just a couple kids. They're no threat," Jimmy hastily answered.

"Obviously they are...they are in my *secret* facility!" Roslun grabbed Jimmy's radio and screamed into it, "Get them out now!"

Jimmy stayed on the elevator when the doors opened. "I will go make sure they are taken care of."

"Hurry up!" Roslun's face was twisted with rage as the elevator doors closed.

Back in the security office, Jimmy looked at the monitors and assessed the situation. "Have you dispatched men to their location?"

"Yes, Sir. They should be engaging in about two minutes. Orders are to shoot on sight."

Jimmy turned and hurried out of the security office.

16

"Looks like we're almost there." Gee said looking up at the ceiling.

"How can you tell?" Sam's voice was almost unintelligible

Joshua Cook

through his hand, which still covered his nose and mouth.

"The pipes. When they take a turn to the right, we should be near the ladder." Gee shined the flashlight along the ceiling, following the piping down the tunnel, "There it is." The light stopped on a section of pipe and scanned around, finally resting on a ladder built into the wall.

Gee and Sam ran toward the ladder when a large hand hit Sam in the face, knocking him into the filth. Gee whirled around to see a man standing over Sam with a gun aimed at his head.

"No!" Gee screamed and went for her gun. The bag slipped from Gee's wet hands sending the gun flying onto the ground. Knowing she had to do something, she threw her flashlight. Unable to move out of the way fast enough, the man took the blow in his right eye.

Wobbling a little, the man tried to get a good aim on Gee, who had begun charging at him like a bull in Pamplona. The shot went wide and missed Gee as she lunged forward. Gee and the man both toppled into the sewage, landing on top of Sam. For a moment there was a lot of yelling and scrambling as the three bodies tried to untangle themselves.

"Quick, grab the gun!" Gee yelled.

Sam crawled out from under the other two and through the sludge. Frantically, he ran his hands over the bottom of the sewage tunnel.

"Hurry up!" Gee was trying to keep their attacker down as long as she could, but she was no match for the towering guard.

Sam looked back around to see the guard rising to his feet with Gee hanging at his side like a little child on her mother's hip. Sam searched faster and finally felt the gun underneath his hands. He lifted it out of the sewage and fired at the guard.

Click. Click.

"Shit! It's not firing!" Sam backed up as he continued to pull the trigger.

Click. Click. Click.

"I'm done playing with you two," The guard grabbed Gee from his side and tossed her back into the sewage like a sack of garbage. "You're next," he threatened Sam as he advanced on him.

Gee was lying on the ground and not moving. It was hard to

tell if she was breathing or not, and there was no time to find out. Sam knew if he did not get out of this situation quickly, none of them would be breathing.

With nowhere to run, Sam turned and bolted down the tunnel, trying to put as much distance between him and the guard as he could. With every glance over his shoulder, Sam saw the guard easily closing the gap between them. Further into the tunnels he ran, until he was knocked to the ground again.

Not paying attention to where he was going, Sam didn't notice a pipe hanging just low enough to graze his head. He rolled over just in time to see his attacker standing over him, a piece of metal held above his head.

This is it. I guess I deserve this. I love you, Heather.

Sam closed his eyes, awaiting the blow from the guard's weapon. Instead of that blow, Sam felt a spray of liquid, like a summertime sprinkler, over his body. He opened his eyes and looked around, expecting to see the guard still standing in front of him. Instead he saw the guard lying face down on the ground.

Sam got to his feet and looked himself over. His clothes were stained with blood. As he inched passed the guard, Sam noticed he was shot in the back of the head. That must be why he was covered in blood. It was the guard's. He looked up and down the tunnel, but saw no shooter.

Sam ran back to Gee, who was leaning against the wall ladder holding her head. There was blood dripping down the side of her face. "What the hell happened to you?" She asked.

"Don't worry. It isn't mine." Sam motioned to the blood on his clothes.

"That doesn't really make it any better." Gee struggled to stand on her own.

"I was about to be killed and out of nowhere the mystery gunman saved my life again." Sam had so many emotions all vying trying to get out that he replayed the entire situation out for Gee with theatrical gusto. As he finished up, Sam made sure to ask her, "So are you ok?"

Gee shook her head at him and insisted she was fine as they climbed the ladder.

17

"What do you mean she's gone?" Roslun screamed.

"When we came in to check on her, we found the cell empty." A guard motions to the empty cell around him and Roslun.

Roslun walked out of Alice's empty cell, rubbing his forehead with his forefinger and thumb, "Find her!" The guard ran out of the room followed by the moans and cries of the undead prisoners in the other cells. "Shut the fuck up, all of you!" Roslun grabbed his radio, "Jimmy...Jimmy, where the hell are you?"

Jimmy's reply came over the radio, "I heard gunshots. I'm going to back Mark up. He hasn't come back from the sewer tunnels yet."

"There is too much going on here. I'm heading to the roof. Meet me up there," Roslun set the radio back into his pocket and began heading for the roof. On his way past the security room, an image on one of the monitors caught Roslun's eye. "That son of a bitch!"

18

Jimmy hung up the radio and continued to watch the empty hallway he had been standing in. He looked from one end to the other, seeing no sign of life, "It's clear. Let's move."

He hurried down the hall with Alice close behind. As they reached the end of the hall, he held up his hand, signaling for her to stop. When he was sure it was clear, he looked at Alice, "You need to hurry. Your sister is here to save you."

"Gee's here?!" Alice asked with a childlike eagerness reminiscent of her former self.

"Yes. Head down the hall and turn left. You should run right into them."

Alice glanced down the hall and then back up at Jimmy's face, "Thank you, but I have to ask; why are you helping me?"

Jimmy stared down at Alice's beautiful, green eyes and a smile spread across his face. "I have done a lot of things in my life that I can never forget. I would like at least one of those things to be something good. Now go."

Alice in Zombieland

Jimmy shoved Alice down the hall and took off in the opposite direction. Alice watched him go, and then ran down the hallway he had showed her. So many thoughts were flying around her head as she ran, but only one question kept coming back...*What happened in Seattle?*

"Alice!"

Hearing her name screamed down the hall snapped Alice out of her thoughts, "Gee!" The two sisters ran towards each other, tightly embracing one another as tears rolled down their faces.

"Hey, this is all *After School Special* sweet and all, but we need to leave like now," Sam told the girls.

They snapped out of their hug. "What the hell happened to you?" asked Alice, seeing the blood on his clothes.

Sam sighed and explained what happened, minus any theatrical flair this time. "There. Now that we're all caught up, we have to get out of here."

"He's right. We have to go," Alice agreed.

"But how?" Gee asked, "There are guards everywhere."

"I know how to get out of here."

Sam and Gee both looked at Alice.

"How do you know?" Gee asked.

"I'll explain on the way. Let's go."

The three of them ran down the hall with Alice in the lead. "In here," Alice dipped into a room off the corridor. Inside the room, they noticed garbage strewn all over the ground. Garbage bins lined one wall, while a series of three chutes lined another wall.

"Quick jump in." Alice opened the door to one of the chutes.

"Oh no. I am not playing around in anymore garbage today," Sam protested, "I will never get this stench off me as it is." He folded his arms across his chest stubbornly.

"Really? You want to do this now?!" Gee grabbed Sam and shoved him towards the chute. "If you don't get down that chute, you won't have to worry about the stink of garbage on you...You can be more worried about the smell of death as you get shot for being stupid!"

Realizing there was not much of a choice; Sam decided to brave the garbage chute and dived in head first. Alice and Gee jumped in right behind him.

Joshua Cook

"Ahh!!"

Their screams echoed through the chute as the three of them slid down. With barely enough room to fit, this was no smooth trip. Limbs and heads banged against the walls all the way down. Finally they burst through the end of the chute and landed hard on mounds of garbage.

"Watch the walls!" Sam tried to stand but fell back into a pile of yesterday's lunch.

"Why?" Gee helped Alice to her feet as they both looked around panicked.

"Haven't you ever seen *Star Wars*?" Sam tried to get to his feet, falling into spaghetti once again, "The walls are going to start closing."

"Are you seriously basing life or death decisions on a movie? This is no compactor. It's just a garbage room," Gee told Sam as she grabbed his hand and began pulling. "Now let's get out of here."

"Oh." Sam stood in the doorway, as the girls walked past him. "Well it could have been, you don't know."

"Follow me," Alice led the three of them down another corridor.

"How do you know where you're going?" Gee asked Alice as they rounded a corner.

"A man told me. My cell door opened and a big guy walked in." Alice stopped for a minute to tell her story, "He told me that I had to get out here. He said you were here for me, but you couldn't make it alone," She pointed to her sister. "He didn't tell me you brought somebody with you though," She looked at Sam, who waved in a *Nice to meet* you sort of way.

"So he let you go?" asked Gee.

"Not only let me go, he told me there would be a boat waiting for us."

Gee grabbed Alice's arm as she tried to start down the hall again, "How do you know this isn't a trap?"

"Why would he break me out just to capture me again? Doesn't seem to make a lot of sense, does it? Plus, I'm guessing he is the same guy that helped you guys."

Seeing Alice's point and knowing there really was no other

Alice in Zombieland

choice, Gee followed Alice and Sam down the hall. As they turned another corner, they saw an unmarked door.

"He said this door will be unlocked," Alice tried the door and it opened easily. She smiled and looked back at Gee and Sam, "Let's go."

On the other side of the door was a dark service corridor. There were only a few light bulbs hanging loosely from the ceiling, each one casting a dim glow over the scene. At the very end of the hall was another door. Unfortunately, in front of that door was a very large man.

"Is this our mystery man?" Gee stopped in the middle of the corridor and raised her gun, training it on the unknown figure at the end of the hallway.

"No," The man answered in a deep voice, "but he is being taken care of."

"What's that mean?!" Alice asked. Gee grabbed her sister as she tried to run at the man.

"This is the end of the line for you. Your hero isn't here anymore, little girl." The man laughed as he stepped into the light. He was tall and lanky, with a professionally cut head of brown hair. His clothing suggested that he was heading to a golf outing, not getting ready to kill three people in a dimly lit corridor.

"It's you!" Sam screamed, instantly recognizing Will. "What are you doing?"

"What I was trying to do all along. You were supposed to be dead before you even made it here," Will answered as he continued to advance on the group.

"So this *was* a trap?!" Gee held out her arm to stop Sam from rushing forward.

"I'll fucking kill you!" Sam screamed from behind Gee's arm.

"Oh, no you won't," The calm in Will's voice enraged Sam even more. "That's why I came out here. When Richard never responded to my message, I knew something had happened." Will slowly moved forward as he spoke, "I made it right on time, I'd say."

"On time to die!" Sam was trying to free himself from Gee who had a tight grip on his arm.

There was a shot and Sam fell to the ground screaming.

Joshua Cook

"You shot me!" Sam was holding his right leg as blood oozed onto the ground.

"You'll live... For now," Will laughed.

"If you're going to kill us, then just do it!" Gee screamed as she helped Sam back up, supporting him with her body.

"Oh I'm going to kill you two," Will waved the gun at Gee and Sam, "But *she* is coming back with me." He targeted the gun on Alice's head as he said this last part.

"You will never take her," Gee screamed as she and Sam took a protective stance in front of Alice.

"You're protecting *her*? Now that's funny," A loud laugh filled the dark corridor. "Do you even know what she is?"

"My sister. That's what she will always be." Gee ran at Will before anyone could grab her. Sam fell back to the floor, screaming in pain.

Will swatted her aside like a bug, "Who's next?"

The smirk on Will's face was too much for Alice to handle, "Me."

"Alice, no!" Sam screamed and began digging through Gee's bag which had fallen next to him.

"You know you can't kill me," Alice told Will as she slowly walked forward.

"Shot to the head. You aren't invincible, little girl." Will cocked his gun, which was still aimed between Alice's eyes. She stopped. "One more step and you will die. Twice," Will warned.

Alice stood there, staring directly into Will's brown eyes, "You wouldn't."

"Try me."

Alice took a step and fell as a shot was fired. She looked up to see Will falling to the ground. She turned to the other end of the corridor.

"Help me up, I don't think I killed him," Sam said and held out his hand.

"Where did you get the gun?" Alice asked as she pulled him to his feet.

"From my bag," Gee was stumbling toward her sister. "Now let's go before he gets up."

The girls finished helping Sam to his feet and the three of

Alice in Zombieland

them made their way past the unconscious Will, blood pouring from his chest. Once outside, they easily found a trail leading to the water.

Just as Alice was told, there was a boat waiting for them. It was a small motorboat, but large enough to get the three of them back to the shore safely. They climbed in and Sam started up the engine. The motor hummed to life and he smiled, "Can I give you ladies a lift?"

19

"You made it," Roslun was standing on the roof as Jimmy exited the building. "I've been waiting for you."

"Thank you, Sir." Jimmy walked out onto the roof.

"Don't go thanking me. It's the least I can do for such a loyal and trusted employee." Roslun handed Jimmy an electronic tablet, "I saw an interesting video I think you should watch. Go ahead. Push play."

Jimmy tapped the bright green play button on the blank screen. Instantly it lit up and played back surveillance video of a dark corridor. The corridor was empty, but then two figures ran into view of the camera, and the video paused.

Roslun grabbed the tablet out of Jimmy's hands, "What the fuck were you doing with her?"

"She is only a girl. You have no right," Jimmy angrily answered.

"I have every right. I control everything, and now I control *death* itself. Who is going to tell me what I can't do? Nobody!" Roslun threw the tablet at Jimmy, but missed and watched as it flew over the edge.

"I will," Jimmy steadied himself and pulled his gun.

"You think that little thing is going to hurt me?" Roslun raised his arms into the air and screamed, "Go ahead. Take your best shot!"

Jimmy fired three shots into Roslun's chest, knocking him to the ground.

Slowly Richard Roslun rose to his feet, laughing the whole time. Blood poured out of the three bullet holes in his chest. Suddenly two more shots are fired, this time from behind Roslun. The bullets screamed past Roslun and tore through Jimmy's chest, puncturing his heart and lungs.

As Jimmy fell to his knees, blood gurgling from his mouth like a decorative fountain, Richard Roslun turned and said, "Let's go."

Roslun boarded the chopper and it flew off into the night sky.

About the Author and Thank You's

Joshua Cook is a freelance writer living in the Seattle, Washington, area. Over the years he has written for a number of publications and websites, and has created his first fiction story with the Zombie A.C.R.E.S. series. Thanks to the success of this series, Josh has been able to focus more time on his freelance writing career and spending time with his best friend, Sam Dogg. Sam is a four year old, black lab/cocker spaniel mix – and the greatest dog in the world, according to Josh, at least. For more information on hiring Joshua Cook for your next big project, email him at joshuacookwrites@yahoo.com.

A big special thank you to Michelle Shores and Bradi Conner for their help and support.

About the Editor

Julianne Snow is the author of the zombie web series *Days with the Undead* and blog The Flipside of Julianne. She is also a zombie columnist for The Spirit Digest.

Formatting services by Lyle Perez of TheMadFormatter.com.

In the summer of 2011, I ran a successful funding campaign on Kickstarter. The following are each and every one of the amazing people who believe in me and Zombie A.C.R.E.S. This project has blossomed into a comic series due out soon with Ratatat Graphics. Watch for it online and at conventions across the country. Please visit and support all of the Backers listed below:

Bob Raymond (@walkerBob on Twitter) ~ Jeff Gupton - BlackByrne Publishing ~ Gaming Tonic ~ Chris Baker - Rogue University ~ Matt Polchlopek - Matt's Grindhouse Goodies ~ Mark 'Dinky' Bakula ~ Julianne Snow - Days With the Undead ~ Tony Elliott - Z Roe ~ Storms ~ Gareth Ellis - Todd the Zombie Lizz-Ayn Shaarawi ~ Jesse Dedman - Zombie Hunter ~ Dayzgrl76 ~ Shana Hammaker ~ Bizarre Comics Entertainment ~ Lewis R. Cougill - GenXnerd.com ~ John Scrofani ~ Shawn Beatty - KingZombie.com ~ David - http://by.davidaludwig.com/~ Train Zata - trainzata.com ~ Michael Wirth - Artist/Writer ~ Kelley Wyskiel - Actress ~ Jarod Watson - AlienBobz.com ~ Leona Bushman - Writer/Artist ~ Gavin ap' Morrygan - The Wayne Foundation Charity ~ SlamFist - Mike Stegman ~ Reign Mack - Coder/Gamer ~ Morgan Barnhart - Zombie Response Team ~ 'Dark' Mark Herbrechtsmeier